P9-CET-206

Kathleen regarded Ben with a cheerful expression.

"Any other bets you want to put on the table?"

"Not at the moment," he said, exasperated. "I'll get back to you."

"Yes, I imagine you will." Her smile expanded. "It's nice to know that I now have something *you* want. Sort of levels the playing field, doesn't it?"

"You're a sneaky woman. You know that, don't you?"

"Of course."

"It must be why Destiny has taken to you."

"That's one reason," Kathleen agreed. "The other has a lot to do with this impossible nephew she's trying to marry off."

Ben was surprised that she could joke about that. "I thought you found that idea as terrifying as I do."

Kathleen paused. "Maybe it's growing on me."

Dear Reader,

It's spring, love is in the air…and what better way to celebrate than by taking a break with Silhouette Special Edition? We begin the month with *Treasured*, the conclusion to Sherryl Woods's MILLION DOLLAR DESTINIES series. Though his two brothers have been successfully paired off, Ben Carlton is convinced he's "destined" to go it alone. But the brooding, talented young man is about to meet his match in a beautiful gallery owner—courtesy of fate…plus a little help from his matchmaking aunt.

And Pamela Toth concludes the MERLYN COUNTY MIDWIVES series with *In the Enemy's Arms,* in which a detective trying to get to the bottom of a hospital black-market drug investigation finds himself in close contact with his old high school flame, now a beautiful M.D.—she's his prime suspect! And exciting new author Lynda Sandoval (look for her Special Edition novel *One Perfect Man,* coming in June) makes her debut and wraps up the LOGAN'S LEGACY Special Edition prequels, all in one book—*And Then There Were Three.* Next, Christine Flynn begins her new miniseries, THE KENDRICKS OF CAMELOT, with *The Housekeeper's Daughter,* in which a son of Camelot—Virginia, that is—finds himself inexplicably drawn to the one woman he can never have. Marie Ferrarella moves her popular CAVANAUGH JUSTICE series into Special Edition with *The Strong Silent Type,* in which a female detective finds her handsome male partner somewhat less than chatty. But her determination to get him to talk quickly morphs into a determination to…get him. And in Ellen Tanner Marsh's *For His Son's Sake,* a single father trying to connect with the son whose existence he just recently discovered finds in the free-spirited Kenzie Daniels a woman they could *both* love.

So enjoy! And come back next month for six heartwarming books from Silhouette Special Edition.

Happy reading!

Gail Chasan
Senior Editor

Please address questions and book requests to:
Silhouette Reader Service
U.S.: 3010 Walden Ave., P.O. Box 1325, Buffalo, NY 14269
Canadian: P.O. Box 609, Fort Erie, Ont. L2A 5X3

SHERRYL WOODS

TREASURED

Silhouette®

SPECIAL EDITION®

Published by Silhouette Books

America's Publisher of Contemporary Romance

If you purchased this book without a cover you should be aware
that this book is stolen property. It was reported as "unsold and
destroyed" to the publisher, and neither the author nor the
publisher has received any payment for this "stripped book."

SILHOUETTE BOOKS

RECYCLED PAPER

ISBN 0-373-24609-9

TREASURED

Copyright © 2004 by Sherryl Woods

All rights reserved. Except for use in any review, the reproduction
or utilization of this work in whole or in part in any form by any
electronic, mechanical or other means, now known or hereafter
invented, including xerography, photocopying and recording, or in
any information storage or retrieval system, is forbidden without
the written permission of the editorial office, Silhouette Books,
233 Broadway, New York, NY 10279 U.S.A.

All characters in this book have no existence outside the imagination of
the author and have no relation whatsoever to anyone bearing the same
name or names. They are not even distantly inspired by any individual
known or unknown to the author, and all incidents are pure invention.

This edition published by arrangement with Harlequin Books S.A.

® and TM are trademarks of Harlequin Books S.A., used under license.
Trademarks indicated with ® are registered in the United States Patent
and Trademark Office, the Canadian Trade Marks Office and in other
countries.

Visit Silhouette Books at www.eHarlequin.com

Printed in U.S.A.

Books by Sherryl Woods in Special Edition

Vows
Love #769
Honor #775
Cherish #781
Kate's Vow #823
A Daring Vow #855
A Vow To Love #885

And Baby Makes Three
A Christmas Blessing #1001
Natural Born Daddy #1007
The Cowboy and His Baby #1009
The Rancher and His Unexpected
  Daughter #1016

The Bridal Path
A Ranch for Sara #1083
Ashley's Rebel #1087
Danielle's Daddy Factor #1094

**And Baby Makes Three:
The Next Generation**
The Littlest Angel #1142
Natural Born Trouble #1156
Unexpected Mommy #1171
The Cowgirl and the Unexpected
  Wedding #1208
Natural Born Lawman #1216
The Cowboy and His Wayward Bride #1234
Suddenly, Annie's Father #1268
The Unclaimed Baby

**And Baby Makes Three:
The Delacourts of Texas**
The Cowboy and the New Year's
  Baby #1291
Dylan and the Baby Doctor #1309
The Pint-Sized Secret #1333
Marrying a Delacourt #1352
The Delacourt Scandal #1363

The Calamity Janes
Do You Take This Rebel? #1394
Courting the Enemy #1411
To Catch a Thief #1418
Wrangling the Redhead #1429
The Calamity James

The Devaneys
Ryan's Place #1489
Sean's Reckoning #1495
Michael's Discovery #1513
Patrick's Destiny #1549
Daniel's Desire #1555

Million Dollar Destinies
Isn't It Rich? #1597
Priceless #1603
Treasured #1609

SHERRYL WOODS

has written more than seventy-five novels. She also operates her own bookstore, Potomac Sunrise, in Colonial Beach, Virginia. If you can't visit Sherryl at her store, then be sure to drop her a note at P.O. Box 490326, Key Biscayne, FL 33149 or check out her Web site at www.sherrylwoods.com.

CAST OF CHARACTERS

Ben Carlton—He sees the world with an artist's eye for detail. The youngest and least ambitious of the successful Carlton brothers, he's usually content to let his brothers be the family headliners. But Ben's sensitive soul cries out for someone who shares his vision of the world.

Kathleen Dugan—She doesn't need much coaxing to recognize that Ben is a talented artist and a tortured soul. A successful gallery owner, she sees beauty in his art and fame in his future. But getting Ben to see what she does will take more than a twist of fate. It will take the kind of determination that's her speciality.

Destiny Carlton—She knows that her youngest nephew has been twice burned by tragedy. Convincing him to love again will take every clever trick at her disposal, along with a woman who won't take no for an answer. There's not a doubt in Destiny's mind that she's found just the woman in Kathleen.

**A man who's closed himself off from love,
a woman with heart and Destiny's touch.
It's bound to be picture-perfect.**

Chapter One

It had been one of those Friday-night gallery receptions that made Kathleen Dugan wonder if she'd been wrong not to take a job teaching art in the local school system. Maybe putting finger paints in the hands of five-year-old kids would be more rewarding than trying to introduce the bold, vibrant works of an amazingly talented young artist to people who preferred bland and insipid.

Of course, it hadn't helped that Boris Ostronovich spoke little English and took the temperamental-artist stereotype to new heights. He'd been sulking in a corner for the last two hours, a glass of vodka in one hand and a cigarette in the other. The cigarette had remained unlit only because Kathleen had threatened to close the show if he lit it up in direct defiance of fire codes, no-smoking policies and a whole list of personal objections.

All in all, the evening had pretty much been a disaster. Kathleen was willing to take responsibility for that. She hadn't gauged correctly just how important it was for the artist to mingle and make small talk. She'd thought Boris's work would sell itself. She'd discovered, instead, that people on the fence about a purchase were inclined to pass when they hadn't exchanged so much as a civil word with the artist. In another minute or two, when the few remaining guests had cleared out of her gallery, Kathleen was inclined to join Boris in a good, old-fashioned, well-deserved funk. She might even have a couple of burning shots of straight vodka, assuming there was any left by then.

"Bad night, dear?"

Kathleen turned to find Destiny Carlton regarding her with sympathy. Destiny was not only an artist herself, she was a regular at Kathleen's gallery in historic Old Town Alexandria, Virginia. Kathleen had been trying to wheedle a few of Destiny's more recent paintings from her to sell, but so far Destiny had resisted all of her overtures.

Destiny considered herself a patron of the arts these days, not a painter. She said she merely dabbled on those increasingly rare occasions when she picked up a brush at all. She was adamant that she hadn't done any work worthy of a showing since she'd closed her studio in the south of France over two decades ago.

Despite her disappointment, Kathleen considered Destiny to be a good friend. She could always be counted on to attend a show, if not to buy. And her understanding of the art world and her contacts had proven invaluable time and again as Kathleen worked to get her galley established.

''The worst,'' Kathleen said, something she would never have admitted to anyone else.

''Don't be discouraged. It happens that way sometimes. Not everyone appreciates genius when they first see it.''

Kathleen immediately brightened. ''Then it isn't just me? Boris's work really is incredible?''

''Of course,'' Destiny said with convincing enthusiasm. ''It's just not to everyone's taste. He'll find his audience and do rather well, I suspect. In fact, I was speaking to the paper's art critic before he left. I think he plans to write something quite positive. You'll be inundated with sales by this time next week. At the first whiff of a major new discovery, collectors will jump on the bandwagon, including some of those who left here tonight without buying anything.''

Kathleen sighed. ''Thank you so much for saying that. I thought for a minute I'd completely lost my touch. Tonight was every gallery owner's worst nightmare.''

''Only a momentary blip,'' Destiny assured her. She glanced toward Boris. ''How is he taking it?''

''Since he's barely said two words all evening, even before the night was officially declared a disaster, it's hard to tell,'' Kathleen said. ''Either he's pining for his homeland or he had a lousy disposition even before the show. My guess is the latter. Until tonight I had no idea how important the artist's charm could be.''

Destiny gave her a consoling look. ''In the end it won't matter. In fact, the instant the critics declare Boris a true modern-art genius, all those people he put off tonight will brag to their friends about the night they met the sullen, eccentric artist.''

Kathleen gave Destiny a warm hug. "Thank you so much for staying behind to tell me that."

"Actually, I lingered till the others had gone because I wanted a moment alone with you."

"Oh?"

"What are your plans for Thanksgiving, Kathleen? Are you going to Providence to visit your family?"

Kathleen frowned. She'd had a very tense conversation with her wealthy, socialite mother on that very topic earlier in the day, when she'd announced her intention to stay right here in Alexandria. She'd been reminded that all three current generations of Dugans gathered religiously for all major holidays. She'd been told that her absence was an affront to the family, a precursor to the breakdown of tradition. And on and on and on. It had been incredibly tedious and totally expected, which was why she'd put off making the call until this morning. Prudence Dugan was not put off easily, but Kathleen had held her ground for once.

"Actually I'm staying in town," she told Destiny. "I have a lot of work to catch up on. And I don't really want to close the gallery for the holiday weekend. I think business could be brisk on Friday and Saturday."

Destiny beamed at her. "Then I would love it if you would spend Thanksgiving day with my family. We'll all be at Ben's farm. It's lovely in Middleburg this time of year."

Kathleen regarded her friend suspiciously. While they had become rather well acquainted in recent years, this was the first time Destiny had sought to include her in a family gathering.

"Won't I be intruding?" she asked.

"Absolutely not. It will be a very low-key dinner for family and a few close friends. And it will give you a chance to see my nephew's paintings and give me a professional opinion.''

Kathleen's suspicions mounted. She knew for a fact that Destiny's eye for art was every bit as good as her own. She also knew that Ben Carlton considered his painting to be little more than a hobby, something he loved to do. In fact, as far as she knew, he'd never sold his work. She suspected there was a good reason for that, that even he knew it wasn't of the caliber needed to make a splash in the art world.

Every article she'd ever read about the three Carlton men had said very little about the reclusive youngest brother. Ben stayed out of the spotlight, which shone on businessman and politician Richard Carlton and football great Mack Carlton. There were rumors of a tragic love affair that had sent Ben into hiding, but none of those rumors had ever been publicly confirmed. However, *brooding* was the adjective that was most often applied whenever his name was mentioned.

''Is he thinking of selling his works?'' Kathleen asked carefully, trying to figure out just what her friend was up to. Being first in line for a chance to show them would, indeed, be a major coup. There was bound to be a lot of curiosity about the Carlton who chose to stay out of the public eye, whether his paintings were any good or not.

''Heavens, no,'' Destiny said, though there was a hint of dismay in her voice. ''He's very stubborn on that point, but I'd like to persuade him that a talent like his shouldn't be hidden away in that drafty old barn of a studio out there.''

''And you think I might be able to change his mind when *you* haven't succeeded?'' Kathleen asked, her skepticism plain. Destiny had lots of practice wheedling million-dollar donations to her pet charities. Surely she could persuade her own nephew that he was talented.

"Perhaps. At the very least, you'll give him another perspective. He thinks I'm totally biased."

Never able to resist the chance that she might discover an exciting new talent, Kathleen finally nodded. She assured herself it was because she wanted a glimpse of the work, not the mysterious man. "I'd love to come for Thanksgiving. Where and when?"

Destiny beamed at her. "I'll send over directions and the details first thing in the morning." She headed for the door, looking oddly smug. "Oh, and wear that bright red silk tunic of yours, the one you had on at the Carlucci show. You looked stunning that night."

Destiny was gone before Kathleen could think of a response, but the comment had set off alarm bells. Everyone in certain social circles in the Washington Metropolitan region knew about Destiny's matchmaking schemes. While her behind-the-scenes plots had never made their way into the engagement or wedding announcements for Richard or Mack, they were hot gossip among the well-connected. And everyone was waiting to see what she would do to see Ben take the walk down the aisle.

Kathleen stared after her. "Oh, no, you don't," she whispered to Destiny's retreating back. "I am not looking for a husband, especially not some wounded, artistic type."

It was a type she knew all too well. It was the type she'd married, fought with and divorced. And while that had made her eminently qualified to run an art gallery and cope with artistic temperament, it had also strengthened her resolve never, ever, to be swept off her feet by another artist.

Tim Radnor had been kind and sensitive when they'd first met. He'd adored Kathleen, claiming she was his muse. But when his work faltered, she'd discovered that he had a cruel streak. There had been flashes of temper and stormy torrents of hurtful words. He'd never laid a hand on her, but his verbal abuse had been just as intolerable. Her marriage had been over within months. Healing had taken much longer.

As a result of that tumultuous marriage, she could deal with the craziness when it came to business, but not when it affected her heart.

If romance was on Destiny's mind, she was doomed to disappointment, Kathleen thought, already steeling her resolve. Ben Carlton could be the sexiest, most charming and most talented artist on the planet and it wouldn't matter. She would remain immune, because she knew all too well the dark side of an artistic temperament.

Firm words. Powerful resolve. She had 'em both. But just in case, Kathleen gazed skyward. "Help me out here, okay?"

"Is trouble?" a deep male voice asked quizzically.

Kathleen jumped. She'd forgotten all about Boris. Turning, she faced him and forced a smile. "No trouble, Boris. None at all." She would see to it.

Only a faint, pale hint of sunlight streamed across the canvas, but Ben Carlton was hardly aware that night was falling. It was like this when a painting was nearing completion. All he could see was what was in front of his eyes, the layers of color, the image slowly unfolding, capturing a moment in time, an impression he was terrified would be lost if he let it go before the last stroke was done. When natural light faded, he automatically adjusted the artificial light without really thinking about it.

"I should have known," a faintly exasperated female voice said, cutting through the silence.

He blinked at the interruption. No one came to his studio when he was working, not without risking his wrath. It was the one rule in a family that tended to defy rules.

"Go away," he muttered, his own impatience as evident as the annoyance in his aunt's voice.

"I most certainly will not go away," Destiny said. "Have you forgotten what day this is? What time it is?"

He struggled to hold on to the image in his head, but it fluttered like a snapshot caught by a breeze, then vanished. He sighed, then slowly turned to face his aunt.

"It's Thursday," he said to prove that he was not as oblivious as she'd assumed.

Destiny Carlton gave him a look filled with tolerant amusement. "Any particular Thursday?"

Ben dragged a hand through his hair and tried to remember what might be the least bit special about this particular Thursday. He was not the kind of man who paid attention to details, unless they were the sort of details going into one of his paintings. Then he could remember every nuance of light and texture.

"A holiday," she hinted. "One when the entire family gathers together to give thanks, a family that is currently waiting for their host while the turkey gets cold and the rolls burn."

"Aw, hell," he muttered. "I forgot all about Thanksgiving. Everyone's here already?"

"They have been for some time. Your brothers threatened to eat every bite of the holiday feast and leave you nothing, but I convinced them to let me try to drag you away from your painting." She stepped closer and eyed the canvas with a critical eye. "It's amazing, Ben. No one captures the beauty of this part of the world the way you do."

He grinned at the high praise. "Not even you? You taught me everything I know."

"When you were eight, I put a brush in your hand and taught you technique. You have the natural talent. It's extraordinary. I dabbled. You're a genius."

"Oh, please," he said, waving off the praise.

Painting had always given him peace of mind, a sense of control over the chaotic world around him. When his parents had died in a plane crash, he'd needed to find something that made sense, something that wouldn't abandon him. Destiny had bought him his first set of paints, taken him with her to a sidewalk near the family home on a charming, shaded street in Old Town Alexandria and told him to paint what he saw.

That first crude attempt still hung in the old town house where she continued to live alone now that he and his brothers had moved on with their lives. She insisted it was her most prized possession because it showed the promise of what he could become. She'd squirreled away some of Richard's early business plans and Mack's football trophies for the same reason. Destiny could be cool and calculating when necessary, but for the most part she was ruled by sentiment.

Richard had been clever with money and business.

Mack was athletic. Ben had felt neither an interest in the family company nor in sports. Even when his parents were alive, he'd felt desperately alone, a sensitive misfit in a family of achievers. The day Destiny had handed him those paints, his aunt had given him a sense of pride and purpose. She'd told him that, like her, he brought another dimension to the well-respected family name and that he was never to dismiss the importance of what he could do that the others couldn't. After that, it had been easier to take his brothers' teasing and to dish out a fair amount of his own. He imagined he was going to be in for a ton of it this evening for missing his own party.

Having the holiday dinner at his place in the country had been Destiny's idea. Ben didn't entertain. He knew his way around a kitchen well enough to keep from starving, but certainly not well enough to foist what he cooked on to unsuspecting company. Destiny had dismissed every objection and arrived three days ago to take charge, bringing along the family's longtime housekeeper to clean and to prepare the meal.

If anyone else had tried taking over his life that way, Ben would have rebelled, but he owed his aunt too much. Besides, she understood his need for solitude better than anyone. Ever since Graciela's death, Ben had immersed himself in his art. The canvas and paints didn't make judgments. They didn't place blame. He could control them, as he couldn't control his own thoughts or his own sense of guilt over Graciela's accident on that awful night three years ago.

But if Destiny understood all that, she also seemed to know instinctively when he'd buried himself in his work for too long. That's when she'd dream up some excuse to take him away from his studio and draw him back into the real world. Tonight's holiday celebration was meant to be one of those occasions. Her one slipup had been not reminding him this morning that today was the day company was coming.

"Give me ten minutes," he told her now. "I'll clean up."

"Too late for that. Melanie is pregnant and starving. She'll eat the flower arrangement if we don't offer an alternative soon. Besides, the company is beginning to wonder if we've just taken over some stranger's house. They need to meet you. You'll make up in charm what you lack in sartorial splendor."

"I have paint on my clothes," he protested, then gave her a hard look as what she'd said finally sank in. "Company? You mean besides Richard and Mack and their wives? Did you say anything about company when you badgered me into having Thanksgiving here?"

"I'm sure I did," she said blithely.

She hadn't, and they both knew it, which meant she was scheming about something more than relieving his solitude. When they reached the house, Ben immediately understood what she was up to.

"And, darling, this is Kathleen Dugan," Destiny said, after introducing several other strangers who were part of the rag-tag group of people Destiny had collected because she knew they had no place else to spend the holiday. There was little question, judging from her tone, that this Kathleen was the pièce de résistance.

He gave his aunt a sharp look. Kathleen was young, beautiful and here alone, which suggested she was available. He'd known for some time now—since Mack's recent wedding, in fact—that Destiny had targeted him for her next matchmaking scheme. Here was his proof—a woman with a fringe of black hair in a pixie cut that emphasized her cheekbones and her amazing violet eyes. There wasn't an artist on earth who wouldn't want to capture that interesting, angular face on canvas. Not that Ben ever did portraits, but even he was tempted to break his hard-and-fast rule. She was stunning in a red silk tunic that skimmed over a slender figure. She wore it over black pants and accented it with a necklace of chunky beads in gold and red. The look was elegant and just a touch avant-garde.

"Lovely to meet you," Kathleen said with a soft smile that showed no hint of the awkwardness Ben was feeling. Clearly she hadn't caught on to the scheme yet.

Ben nodded. He politely shook her hand, felt a startling jolt of awareness, then took another look into her eyes to see if she'd felt the same little *zing*. She showed no evidence of it, thank heavens.

"If you'll excuse my totally inappropriate attire," Ben said, quickly turning away from her and addressing the others, "I gather dinner is ready to be served."

"We've time for another drink," Destiny insisted, apparently no longer worried about the delayed meal. "Richard, bring your brother something. He can spend at least a few minutes socializing before we sit down to eat."

Ben frowned at her. "I thought we were in a rush."

"Only to drag you in here," his very pregnant sister-in-law said as she came and linked an arm through his, drawing him out of the spotlight, even as she whispered conspiratorially, "Don't you know that you're the main attraction?"

He gave Melanie a sharp look. They'd formed a bond back when Richard had been fighting his attraction to her. Ben trusted her instincts. He wanted to hear her take on this gathering. "Oh?"

"You never come out of this lair of yours," Melanie explained. "When Destiny invited us here, we figured something was up."

"Oh?" he said again, waiting to see if she'd drawn the same conclusion about Kathleen's presence here that he had. "Such as?"

Melanie studied him intently. "You really don't know what Destiny is up to? You're as much in the dark as the rest of us?"

Ben glanced toward Kathleen, then. "Not as much as you might think," he said with a faint scowl.

Melanie gave the newcomer a knowing look. "Ah, so that's it. I wondered when Kathleen arrived if she was the chosen one. I figured it was going to be your turn soon. Destiny won't be entirely happy until all of her men are settled."

"I hope you're wrong about that," Ben said darkly. "I'd hate to disappoint her, but I am settled."

Richard overheard him and chuckled. "Oh, bro, if that's what you think, you're delusional." He, too, glanced toward Kathleen, whose head was tilted as she listened intently to something Destiny was saying. "I give you till May."

"June," Mack chimed in. "Destiny's been moping because none of us had a traditional June wedding. You're all she's got left, little brother. She won't allow you to let her down. I caught her out in the garden earlier. I think she was mentally seating the guests and envisioning the perfect area for the reception."

Ben shuddered. Richard and Mack had once been as fiercely adamant about not getting married as he was. Look at the two of them now. Richard even had a baby on the way, and Mack and Beth were talking about adopting one of the sick kids she worked with at the hospital. Maybe more. To his astonishment, those two seemed destined for a houseful. By this time next year, there would be the cries of children filling this house and any other place the Carlton family gathered. No one needed him adding to the clutter. He doubted Destiny saw it that way, though.

There were very few things that Ben wouldn't do for his aunt. Getting married was one of them. He liked his solitude. After the chaotic upheaval of his early years, he counted on the predictability of his quiet life in the country. Graciela had given him a reprieve from that, but then she, too, had died, and it had reinforced his commitment to go through life with his heart under the tightest possible wraps. Those who wrote that he was prone to dark moods and eccentricities had gotten it exactly right. There would be no more nicks in his armor, no more devastating pain to endure.

His resolve steady and sure, he risked another look at Kathleen Dugan, then belatedly saw the smug expression on his aunt's face when she caught him.

Ben sighed, then stood a little straighter, stiffening his spine, giving Destiny a daunting look. She didn't bat so much as an eyelash. That was the trouble with his aunt. She rarely took no for an answer. She was persuasive and sneaky. If he didn't take a firm stand right here, right now, he was doomed.

Unfortunately, though, he couldn't think of a single way to make his position clear over turkey and dressing.

He could always say, "So glad you could come, Kathleen, but don't get any ideas."

Or, "Delighted to meet you, Ms. Dugan, but ignore

every word out of my aunt's mouth. She's devious and clever and not to be trusted.''

Or maybe he should simply say nothing at all, just ignore the woman and avoid his aunt. If he could endure the next couple of hours, they'd all be gone and that would be that. He could bar the gates and go back into seclusion.

Perfect, he concluded. That was definitely the way to go. No overt rudeness that would come back to haunt him. No throwing down of the gauntlet. Just passive acceptance of Kathleen's presence here tonight.

Satisfied with that solution, he turned his attention to the drink Richard had thrust in his hand. A sniff reassured him it was nonalcoholic. He hadn't touched a drop of anything stronger than beer since the night of Graciela's accident.

''Darling,'' Destiny said, her gaze on him as she crossed the room, Kathleen at her side. ''Did I mention earlier that Kathleen owns an art gallery?''

Next to him Melanie choked back a laugh. Richard and Mack smirked. Ben wanted nothing more than to pummel his brothers for getting so much enjoyment out of his discomfort at his aunt's obvious ploy. Kathleen was her handpicked choice for him, all right. There was no longer any question about that.

''Really?'' he said tightly.

''She has the most amazing work on display there now,'' Destiny continued blithely. ''You should stop by and take a look.''

Ben cast a helpless look in Kathleen's direction. She now looked every bit as uncomfortable as he felt. ''Maybe I will one of these days.'' When hell freezes over, he thought even as he muttered the polite words.

"I'd love to have your opinion," Kathleen said gamely.

"My opinion's not worth much," Ben said. "Destiny's the family expert."

Kathleen held his gaze. "But most artists have an eye for recognizing talent," she argued.

Ben barely contained a sigh. Surely Kathleen was smart enough not to fall into his aunt's trap. He wanted to warn her to run for her life, to skip the turkey, the dressing and the pumpkin pie and head back to Alexandria as quickly as possible and bar the door of her gallery from anyone named Carlton. He was tempted to point to Melanie and Beth and explain how they'd unwittingly fallen in with his aunt's schemes, but he doubted his sisters-in-law would appreciate the suggestion that their marriages were anything other than heaven-sent. They both seemed to have revised history to their liking after the wedding ceremonies.

Instead he merely said, "I'm not an artist."

"Of course you are," Destiny declared indignantly. "An exceptionally talented one at that. Why would you say such a thing, Ben?"

To get out of being drawn any further into this web, he very nearly shouted. He looked his aunt in the eye. "Are you an artist?"

"Not anymore," she said at once.

"Because you no longer paint?" he pressed.

Destiny frowned at him. "I still dabble."

"Then it must be because you don't show or sell your work," he said. "Is that why you're no longer an artist?"

"Yes," she said at once. "That's it exactly."

He gave Destiny a triumphant look. "Neither do I. No shows. No sales. I dabble." He found himself wink-

ing at Kathleen. "I guess we can forget about me offering a professional opinion on your current show."

A grin tugged at the corners of Kathleen's mouth.
"Clever," she praised.

"Too clever for his own good," Destiny muttered.

"Uh-oh," Mack murmured, grinning broadly.
"You've done it now, Ben. Destiny's on the warpath.
You're doomed."

Funny, Ben thought, glancing around the room at the
sea of amused expressions, that was the same conclusion he'd reached about an hour ago. He should have
quit back then and saved himself the aggravation.

Chapter Two

Kathleen felt as if the undercurrents swirling around Ben Carlton's living room were about to drag her under. Every single suspicion she'd had about the real reason she'd been invited tonight was being confirmed with every subtle dig, every dark look between Ben and his aunt. Even his brothers and sisters-in-law seemed to be in on the game and were enjoying it thoroughly. In fact, she was the only one who didn't seem to get the rules. If she could have fled without appearing unbearably rude, she might have.

"Would you like to freshen up before dinner?" Beth Carlton asked, regarding her with sympathy.

If it meant escaping from this room, Kathleen would have agreed to join a trek across the still-green fields of winter wheat that stretched as far as the eye could see.

"Yes, please," she said gratefully.

"I'll show you where the powder room is," Beth said.

The minute they were out of earshot of the others, Beth gave her a warm smile. "Feel as if you're caught in an intricate web you didn't even realize was being spun?"

Kathleen nodded. "Worse, I have no idea how I got there. Am I some sort of sacrificial lamb?"

"Pretty much," Beth said. "Believe me, Melanie and I know exactly how you feel. We've been there. We were tangled up with Carlton men before we knew it."

"I don't suppose there's a way out?" Kathleen asked.

"Obviously neither of us found one," Beth said cheerfully. "Maybe you'll be the exception. Right now she's batting two for two, but Destiny's track record is bound to falter sooner or later."

Kathleen studied the pediatric oncologist who'd married Mack. Beth Carlton struck her as quiet, intelligent and lovely in an understated way, very much the opposite of Kathleen's eccentricity and flamboyance. It was hard to imagine that the same woman would have chosen them as potential marriage material for beloved nephews. Then, again, Ben was a far cry from his more outgoing, athletic brother. Destiny obviously knew her nephews well. As Beth had just noted, her knack for choosing the right women was outstanding.

"Then I'm not crazy," Kathleen ventured carefully. "Destiny is plotting to set me up with Ben? She didn't get me out here just to look at his art?"

Beth's grin spread. "Have you actually seen a single canvas since you arrived?"

"No."

"Were you asked to tag along when Destiny went to fetch Ben from his studio?"

"No."

Beth took a little bow, her expression amused. "I rest my case."

"But why me?" Kathleen couldn't keep the plaintive note out of her voice.

"Believe me, I asked the same thing when I realized what Destiny was up to with me and Mack. He was a professional football player, for heaven's sakes, and I'd never even watched a game. At least you and Ben have art in common. On the surface you're a much better match than Mack and I were."

"But Destiny got it right with the two of you, didn't she?" Kathleen concluded.

"Exactly right," Beth admitted happily. "She was absolutely on target with Richard and Melanie, too, though they fought it just as hard as Mack and I did. My advice is to go with the flow and see what happens. Assuming you ever want to get married, maybe having a woman with Destiny's intuition in your corner is not all bad."

"But I'm not looking for a husband," Kathleen protested. "Especially not an artist. I was married to one once. It did not turn out well."

Beth's expression turned thoughtful. "Does Destiny know about that?"

Kathleen shook her head. "I doubt it. I don't talk about it, and I took back my maiden name after the divorce."

"Let me think about this a minute," Beth said, then gestured toward a door. "The powder room's in there. I'll wait right here to show you the way to the dining room."

When Kathleen emerged a few minutes later, she found Beth and Melanie huddled together. They glanced up and beamed at her.

"So, here's the way we see it," Beth said. "Either Destiny knows about your past and figures that will make you a real challenge for Ben."

"Or she's made a serious miscalculation," Melanie said, grinning. "I like that one. Just once I'd like to see her get it wrong. No offense."

"None taken," Kathleen said, liking these two women immensely. She had a feeling their advice was going to be invaluable if she was to evade Destiny Carlton's snare. With any luck Ben would be equally appalled by this scheme, and the whole crazy thing would die for lack of participation by either one of them. He certainly hadn't looked especially happy earlier.

"We'd better go in to dinner before Destiny comes looking for us," Beth said, casting a worried look in the direction of the living room. "Destiny's allowed her conspiracies. Ours make her nervous."

"Why is that?" Kathleen asked.

"Because we're on to her," Melanie explained. "She was terrified I'd warn Beth away. Now she's equally worried that we might gang up and help you escape her clutches. I think she anticipates that the day will come when we'll get even with her, even though we're happy about the outcome of her machinations." She gave Kathleen the same sort of sympathetic look Beth had given her earlier. "We will, you know. If you need backup, just holler. We love Ben and we want to see him happy, but we also feel a certain amount of loyalty to any woman caught up in one of Destiny's matchmaking plots. It's a sisterhood thing."

Kathleen listened to the offer with amusement. Now that she'd been forewarned about the lengths to which Destiny might go, she felt much more confident that she was prepared to deal with her. "Don't worry. I think I can handle Destiny."

The declaration drew hoots of laughter. Despite her confidence in her own willpower and strength, that laughter gave Kathleen pause. That was the voice of experience responding. Two voices, in fact.

"Maybe I'd better get your phone numbers, just in case," she said as they walked toward the dining room where the other guests had now assembled.

In the doorway, Destiny gave them all a sharp look, then beamed at Kathleen. "Come, dear, I've seated you next to Ben."

Of course she had, Kathleen thought, fighting a renewed surge of panic. She avoided glancing at Melanie or Beth, afraid of the justifiable amusement she'd likely find in their eyes now. Instead she cast a look in Ben's direction, wondering what he thought of his aunt's blatant machinations. He had to find them as disquieting as she did.

Oddly enough, she thought he looked surprisingly relaxed. Maybe he was confident of his own ability to resist whatever trap Destiny was setting. Or maybe he hadn't figured out what she was up to. Doubtful, though, if he'd watched his brothers get snared one by one.

Kathleen took a closer look. He was every bit as handsome as she'd expected after seeing his brothers' pictures in the gossip columns of the local papers. There was no mistaking the fact that he was an artist, though. There were paint daubs in a variety of colors on his old jeans, a streak of vermilion on his cheek.

Kathleen couldn't help feeling a faint flicker of admiration for a man who could be so totally unselfconscious showing up at his own dinner party at less than his best.

What a contrast that was to her own insecurities. She'd spent her entire life trying to put her best foot forward, trying to impress, trying to overcome an upbringing that had been financially privileged but beyond that had had very little to redeem it. She'd spent a lifetime hiding secrets and shame, acceding to her mother's pleas not to rock the family boat. Art had brought beauty into her life, and she admired and respected those who could create it.

As she stepped into the dining room, her gaze shifted from Ben to the magnificent painting above the mantel. At the sight of it, she came to a sudden stop. All thoughts of Ben Carlton, Destiny's scheming and her own past flew out of her head. Her breath caught in her throat.

"Oh, my," she whispered.

The artist had captured the fall scene with both a brilliant use of color and a delicate touch that made it seem almost dreamlike, the way it might look in the mind's eye when remembered weeks or months later, too perfect to be real. There was a lone deer at the edge of a brook, traces of snow on the ground with leaves of gold, red and burnished bronze falling along with the last faint snowflakes. The deer was staring straight out of the painting, as if looking directly at the artist, but its keen eyes were serene and unafraid. Kathleen imagined it had been exactly like that when the artist had come upon the scene, then made himself a part of it in a way that protected and preserved the moment.

Destiny caught her rapt gaze. "One of Ben's. He

hated it when I insisted he hang it in here where his guests could enjoy it.''

"But it's spectacular,'' Kathleen said, dismayed that it might have been hidden away if not for Destiny's insistence. Work this amazing did belong in a gallery. "I feel as if I looked out a window and saw exactly that scene.''

Destiny smiled, her expression smug. "I just knew you would react that way. Tell my nephew that, please. He might actually believe it if it comes from you. He dismisses whatever I say. He's convinced I'm biased about his talent.''

Excitement rippled through Kathleen. Destiny hadn't been exaggerating about her nephew's extraordinary gift. "There are more like this?'' she asked, knowing the answer but hardly daring to hope that this was the rule, rather than the exception.

"His studio is packed to the rafters,'' Destiny revealed. "He's given a few to family and friends when we've begged, but for the most part, this is something he does strictly for himself.''

"I could make him rich,'' Kathleen said with certainty, eager to fight to do just that. She was well-known for overcoming objections, for persuading tight-fisted people to part with their money, and difficult artists to agree to showings in her small but prestigious gallery. All of Destiny's scheming meant nothing now. All that mattered was the art.

Destiny squeezed her hand. "Ben is rich. You'll have to find some other lure, if you hope to do a showing.''

"Fame?'' What painter didn't secretly yearn to be this generation's Renoir or Picasso? Disclaimers aside, surely Ben had an artist's ego.

Destiny shook her head. "He thinks Richard and Mack have all the limelight that the Carlton family needs."

Frustration burned inside Kathleen. What else could she come up with that might appeal to a reclusive artist who had no need for money or fame?

She drew her gaze from the incredible painting and turned to the woman who knew Ben best. "Any ideas?" she asked Destiny.

The older woman patted her hand and gave her a serene, knowing look. "I'm sure you'll think of something if you put your mind to it."

Even though she'd suspected the plot all along, even though Melanie and Beth had all but confirmed it, Kathleen was taken aback by the determined glint in Destiny's eyes. In Destiny's mind the art and the man were intertwined. Any desire for one was bound to tie Kathleen to the other. It was a diabolical scheme.

Kathleen looked from the painting to Ben Carlton. She would gladly sell her soul to the devil for a chance to represent such incredible art. But if she was understanding Destiny's sly hint correctly, it wasn't her soul she was expected to sell.

One more glance at Ben, one more little frisson of awareness and she couldn't help thinking it might not be such a bad bargain.

Ben watched warily as his aunt guided Kathleen into the dining room. He saw the way the younger woman came to a sudden halt when she saw his painting, and despite his claim that he painted only for himself, his breath snagged in his throat as he tried to gauge her reaction. She seemed impressed, but without being able to hear what she said, he couldn't be sure. It irked him that he cared.

"You're amazingly talented," Kathleen said the instant she'd taken her seat beside him.

Relief washed over him. Because that annoyed him, too, he merely shrugged. "Thanks. That's Destiny's favorite."

"She has a good eye."

"Have you ever seen *her* work?"

"A few pieces," Kathleen said. "She won't let me sell them for her, though." She met his gaze. "Modesty must run in the family."

"I'm not modest," Ben assured her. "I'm just not interested in turning this into a career."

"Why not?"

His gaze challenged her. "Why should I? I don't need the money."

"Critical acclaim?"

"Not interested."

"Really?" she asked skeptically. "Or are you afraid your work won't measure up?"

He frowned at that. "Measure up to what? Some other artist's? Some artificial standard for technique or style or commercial success?"

"All of that," she said at once.

"None of it matters to me."

"Then why do you paint?"

"Because I enjoy it."

She stared at him in disbelief. "And that's enough?"

He grinned at her astonishment. "Isn't there anything you do, Ms. Dugan, just for the fun of it?"

"Of course," she said heatedly. "But you're wasting your talent, hiding it away from others who could take pleasure in seeing it or owning it."

He was astounded by the assessment. "You think I'm being selfish?"

"Absolutely."

Ben looked into her flashing violet eyes, and for an instant he lost his train of thought, lost his desire to argue with her. If they'd been alone, he might have been tempted to sweep her into his arms and kiss her until she forgot all about this silly debate over whether art was important if it wasn't on display for the masses.

"What are you passionate about?" he asked instead, clearly startling her.

"Art," she said at once.

"Nothing else?"

She flushed at the question. "Not really."

"Too bad. Don't you think that's taking a rather limited view of the world?"

"That from a man who's known far and wide as a recluse?" she retorted wryly.

Ben chuckled. "But a *passionate* recluse," he told her. "I love nature. I care about my family. I feel strongly about what I paint." He shot a look toward Richard. "I'm even starting to care just a little about politics." He turned toward Mack. "Not so much about football, though."

"Only because you could never catch a pass if your life had depended on it," Mack retorted amiably. He grinned at Kathleen. "He was afraid of breaking his fingers and not being able to hold a paint brush again."

"Then, even as a boy you loved painting?" Kathleen said. "It's always mattered to you?"

"It's what I enjoy doing," Ben confirmed. "It's not who I am."

"No ambition at all?"

He shook his head. "Sorry. None. Richard and Mack have more than enough for one family."

Kathleen set down her fork and regarded him with consternation. "How do you define yourself, if not as an artist?"

"A *reclusive* artist," Ben corrected, quoting the usual media description. "Why do I need to pin a label on myself?"

She seemed taken aback by that. "I don't suppose you do."

"How do you define who you are?" he asked.

"I own an art gallery. A very prestigious art gallery, in fact," she said with pride.

Ben studied her intently. He wondered if she had any idea how telling it was that she saw herself only in terms of what she did, not as a woman with any sort of hopes and dreams. A part of him wanted to unravel that particular puzzle and discover what had made her choose ambition over any sort of personal connection.

Because right here and now, surrounded by people absorbed in their own conversations, it was safe enough to ask, he gazed into her amazing eyes. "No man in your life?"

A shadow flitted across her face. "None."

"Why is that?"

Eyes flashing, she met his gaze. "Is there a woman in yours?"

Ben laughed. "Touché."

"Which isn't an answer, is it?"

"No, there is no woman in my life," he said, waiting for the twinge of guilt that usually accompanied that admission.

"Why not?" she asked, proving she was better at the game than he was.

"Because the only one who ever mattered died," he said quietly.

Sympathy immediately filled her eyes. "I'm sorry. I didn't know."

"I'm surprised Destiny didn't fill you in," he said, glancing in his aunt's direction. Though Destiny was engaged in conversation with Richard, it was obvious she was keeping one ear attuned to what was going on between him and Kathleen. She gave him a quizzical look.

"Nothing," Ben said for her benefit. He almost regretted letting the conversation veer away from the safe topic of art. But since Kathleen had sidestepped his question as neatly as he'd initially avoided hers, he went back to it. "Why is there no special man in your life?"

"I was married once. It didn't work out."

There was a story there. He could see it in her face, hear it in the sudden tension in her voice. "Was it so awful you decided never to try it again?"

"Worse," she said succinctly. She met his gaze. "We were doing better when we were sticking to art."

Ben laughed. "Yes, we were, weren't we? I was just thinking the same thing, though I imagine there are those who think all the small talk is just avoidance."

"Avoidance?"

"Two people dancing around what really matters."

Kathleen flushed. "I'm perfectly willing to avoid delving into my personal life. How about you?"

"Suits me," he said easily, though a part of him was filled with regret. "Want to debate about the talent of the Impressionists versus the Modernists?"

She frowned. "Not especially."

"Know anything about politics?"

"Not much."

"Environmental issues?"

"I think global warming is a real risk," she said at once.

"Good for you. Anything else?"

She held up a forkful of turkey. "The food's delicious."

"I was thinking more in terms of another environmental issue," he teased.

"Sorry. You're fresh out of luck. I could argue the merits of free-range turkey over the frozen kind," she suggested cheerfully. "Everyone says free-range is healthier, but they're just as dead, so how healthy is that?"

Ben chuckled. "Now there's a hot-button topic, if ever I heard one."

"You don't have to be sarcastic," she said. "I told you I have a one-track mind."

"And it's totally focused on art," Ben said. "I think I get that." He studied her thoughtfully. "This man you were married to, was he an artist?"

She stiffened visibly. "As a matter of fact, he was."

Ben should have taken comfort in that. If an artist had hurt Kathleen so badly that she wasn't the least bit interested in marriage, then he should be safe enough from all of Destiny's clever machinations. She'd miscalculated this time. Oddly, though, he didn't feel nearly as relieved as he should. In fact, he felt a powerful urge to go find this man who'd hurt Kathleen and wring his neck.

"People get over bad marriages and move on," he told her quietly.

"Have you gotten over losing the woman you loved?"

"No, but it's different."

"Different how?"

Ben hesitated. They were about to enter into an area he never discussed, not with anyone. Somehow, though, he felt compelled to tell Kathleen the truth. "I blame myself for her death," he said.

Kathleen looked momentarily startled by the admission. "Did you cause her death?"

He smiled sadly at the sudden hint of caution in her voice. "Not the way you mean, no, but I was responsible just the same."

"How?"

"We argued. She was drunk and I let her leave. She ran her car into a tree and died." He recited the bare facts without emotion, watching Kathleen's face. She didn't flinch. She didn't look shocked or horrified. Rather she looked indignant.

"You can't blame yourself for that," she said fiercely. "She was an adult. She should have known better than to get behind the wheel when she was upset and drunk."

"People who are drunk are not known for their logic. I could have stopped her. I *should* have," Ben countered as he had to every other person who'd tried to let him off the hook.

"Really? How? By taking away the car keys?"

"That would have done it," he said bleakly, thinking how simple it would have been to prevent the tragedy that had shaped the last three years of his adult life.

"Or she would have waited a bit, then found your keys and taken your car," Kathleen countered.

"It might have slowed her down, though, given her time to think."

"As you said yourself, it doesn't sound to me as if she was thinking all that rationally."

Ben sighed. No, Graciela hadn't been thinking rationally, but neither had he. He'd known her state of mind was irrational that night, that she was feeling defensive and cornered at having been caught with her lover. He'd told her to get out anyway. Not only hadn't he taken those car keys from her, he'd all but tossed her out the door and put her behind the wheel.

"It hardly matters now," he said at last. "I can't change that night."

Kathleen looked directly into his eyes. "No," she said softly. "You can't. The only thing you can do—the thing you *must* do—is put it behind you."

Ben wanted desperately to accept that, to let go of the past as his entire family had urged him to do, but blaming himself was too ingrained. Absolution from a woman he'd known a few hours counted for nothing.

He forced his gaze away from Kathleen and saw Destiny and his brothers watching him intently, as if they'd sensed or even heard what Ben and Kathleen had been discussing and were awaiting either an explosion or a sudden epiphany. He gave them neither.

Instead, he lifted his glass of water. "To good company and wonderful food. Thanks, Destiny."

"To Destiny," the others echoed.

Destiny beamed at him, evidently satisfied that things were working out exactly as she'd intended. "Happy Thanksgiving, everyone."

Ben drank to her toast, but even as he wished everyone a wonderful Thanksgiving, he couldn't help wondering when this dark, empty hole inside him would go away and he'd truly be able to count his blessings again. He gazed at Kathleen and thought he saw shadows in her eyes, as well, and guessed she was feeling much the same way.

He knew Destiny wanted something to come from this meeting today, but it wasn't in the cards. Whatever the whole story, Kathleen Dugan's soul was as shattered as his own.

Chapter Three

Kathleen waited impatiently through several courses of excellent food. She nibbled on pecan pie, then lingered over two cups of rich, dark coffee, hoping for an invitation to Ben's studio to go through the works that were stashed there. She desperately wanted to see for herself if the painting in the dining room was the exception or the rule.

Then again, it might be sheer torment, especially if each and every painting was extraordinary and Ben still flatly refused to allow her to show them.

When the meal finally ended and people started making their excuses and leaving, she lingered at the table with the family. She debated simply asking for a tour of the studio, but Ben's forbidding expression stopped her. Not even Destiny seemed inclined to broach the very subject that she claimed had been her reason for asking Kathleen to dinner. It was as if she, too, had read her nephew's mood and determined that he wouldn't be receptive.

Kathleen was about to accept a momentary defeat and leave, when Melanie stepped in.

"Kathleen, surely you're not going without looking at Ben's paintings," Melanie said, merriment sparkling in her eyes. "Isn't that why you came tonight?"

Ben looked as if he'd like to strangle his sister-in-law. Kathleen took her cue from that.

"Perhaps another time," she said before Ben could utter a word. She smiled at him. "I would love to come back sometime to see your studio, if you'll let me."

He regarded her with a faint frown. "Sure," he said, too polite to refuse outright.

"I'll call to set it up," Kathleen promised. She had no intention of doing that. She had a hunch she needed the element of surprise on her side. Meantime, though, let him get complacent, thinking that he'd have fair warning.

"There's no phone in the studio," Melanie chimed in.

"And Ben never checks his messages," Beth added.

"You should probably just pop in whenever the mood strikes," Melanie suggested.

Kathleen grinned. Obviously those two were on the same wavelength. They'd found a way to encourage her and warn Ben at the same time. Very clever.

"Perhaps I will," Kathleen said. She gave him a pointed look. "If Ben doesn't return my calls."

He rolled his eyes. "I return my calls." He gave his sisters-in-law a hard look. "At least to anyone important."

The two women laughed, not the least bit insulted by the innuendo.

"I guess you put us in our place," Melanie said, giving him a kiss. "Don't be a stranger. I expect you to come to dinner soon."

To Kathleen's surprise, his expression softened and he rested a hand on Melanie's huge belly. "I'd better hurry before this little one steals all your attention."

"We'll always have time for you," Melanie told him. "And we're counting on you to give the baby its first set of paints and plenty of free art lessons, just the way Destiny did for you. Mack's going to teach the baby the finer points of football."

"Even if it's a girl?" Ben inquired skeptically.

"There will be no gender discrimination in this family," Melanie retorted. "Right, Mack?"

"None," Mack agreed at once. "And if it is a girl and she's really, really good, I'll make her the first woman in the National Football League. Who cares about a few cuts and bruises and broken bones?"

"Hold it," Richard said, scowling at his brother. "Nobody gets to tackle any daughter of mine."

Beth nudged Mack in the ribs. "You knew your brother would forbid it, didn't you? Obviously you inherited Destiny's sneakiness. You sound very broadminded since there's absolutely no risk that you'll ever have to pay up."

"Hey, my offer was genuine," Mack insisted, looking hurt that his wife would think otherwise. "Now let's get out of here. We've got some kids at the hospital we want to see tonight. I promised them pie for dessert."

Destiny stood up at once. "I have the pies all ready in the kitchen. I'll get them."

Melanie and Richard left as Mack, Beth and Destiny headed for the kitchen, leaving Kathleen alone with Ben.

"You have an amazing family," she told him.

"They're good people," Ben agreed, then regarded her curiously. "What about your family? Were they together today?"

"Of course. It's tradition." She knew there was no mistaking the harsh edge in her voice, but she was unable to contain it.

"But you weren't there," he noted.

"I'd had enough of tradition," she said succinctly. "I decided it was time to do my own thing."

"Something tells me there's a story there," he said.

"Not a very interesting one," she insisted, unwilling to air the Dugan family laundry to this man she barely knew.

He studied her so intently that she felt herself flush under his scrutiny.

"If you ever change your mind, I'm a good listener," he said eventually.

Kathleen didn't talk about that part of her past any more than she talked about her marriage. "I'll keep that in mind," she said with no intention of following up on it. Why reveal intimate secrets to a man she wanted to represent, not to date? Not that she'd ever shared any part of her family history with anyone. Keeping quiet had been ingrained in her from an early age.

"But you have no intention of talking to me about that or anything else personal, do you?" Ben guessed. "It's all about the art with you."

"Yes," she said, seeing little point in denying it.

"Even if I were to tell you that I'd let you take a look around my studio, if you'd open up to me?"

She gave him a sharp look. "Why would you do that?"

"I'm not sure," he responded slowly, looking faintly bewildered. "Maybe because I'm as fascinated with what you're holding back as you are with the paintings I'm keeping from you."

Kathleen was caught completely off guard by the admission. It was an opening, a chance to get what she wanted, but at what cost?

"I don't think so," she said at last.

"What are you afraid of?"

She wasn't about to answer that. She couldn't tell him that talking about the past would make her far too vulnerable, that it would create an illusion of intimacy that could be far too dangerous. There had been so many times in her life when she'd wanted to share all the secrets, to lean on someone stronger, but she'd kept her own counsel instead, because that was what Dugans did, damn them all.

"I'm not afraid of anything," she said fiercely, desperately wishing it were true. She was terrified of shadows, of people who weren't what they first seemed to be. Her faith in people, her trust had been shattered too many times to count, even by the mother and grandparents she was expected to respect and adore.

"Really?" Ben asked skeptically. "Nothing frightens you?"

"Absolutely nothing," she insisted, meeting his gaze, then faltering at the intensity in his blue eyes.

"Then I guess there's no reason at all not to do this," he said, cupping a hand behind her neck and covering her mouth with his own.

Fire shot through Kathleen's veins as if she'd been touched by flame. Every sensible cell in her brain told her to pull away from the heat, but like the moth tempting fate, she moved into the kiss instead, then moaned when Ben was the one who withdrew.

Feeling dazed, she stared into his eyes, saw the confusion and the passion and wondered what the devil had just happened. If anyone else had hit on her so abruptly, with so little warning, she would have been shaking with anger now. To her shock, while she was indeed trembling, it was because that kiss had touched a part of her she'd thought was forever dead.

"Why?" she asked, unable to form a longer, more coherent question. Besides, *why* pretty much covered it.

"I'm asking myself the same thing," Ben admitted. "Maybe I just wanted to challenge that confidence I heard in your voice."

"Or maybe you wanted to prove something to yourself," she responded irritably.

"Such as?"

"That Destiny had gotten it wrong this time."

"My aunt had nothing to do with that kiss," he said heatedly.

"Oh, really? Then you don't care that it was exactly what she was hoping would happen between us?"

"The damn kiss had nothing to do with Destiny," he said again, dragging his hand through his hair. "I am sorry, though. It shouldn't have happened."

Kathleen sighed. She agreed it had been a mistake, but she couldn't seem to regret it the way she knew she should.

"Let's just forget about it," she suggested mildly. "People kiss all the time and it means nothing." At least, other people did. It was a brand-new experience for her to be able to participate in a kiss without wildly overreacting, without a hint of panic clawing at her.

"Exactly," Ben said, sounding relieved.

"I should go. Please tell Destiny that I had a wonderful time. I'm sure I'll see her soon at the gallery."

"Tomorrow morning would be my guess," Ben said wryly.

Kathleen laughed despite herself. "Mine, too."

"Will you tell her about the kiss?"

"Heavens, no. Will you?"

"Are you crazy? Not a chance."

Kathleen looked into his eyes and made a swift decision. "I'm still coming back out here, you know. You haven't scared me off."

He gave her a vaguely chagrined look that told her she'd hit the mark. That kiss had been deliberate, after all, not the wicked impulse he'd wanted her to believe.

He shrugged. "It was worth a shot."

She laughed at having caught him. "I knew it. I knew that was what the kiss was about."

He gave her a long, lingering look that made her toes curl.

"Not entirely," he said, then grinned. "That should give you something to think about before you get into your car and head out this way again."

It was a dare, no question about it. If only he'd known Kathleen better, he'd have realized that it was a point of honor with her never to resist a challenge. She'd survived her past, and when she'd come through it, she'd vowed never to let another soul intimidate her or get the upper hand. She didn't intend to let Ben Carlton—despite his sexy looks, killer smile and devastating kisses—be the exception.

* * *

After that potent kiss, Ben was surprised and oddly disgruntled when Kathleen simply grabbed her coat and walked out without even waiting to say goodbye to Destiny or to Mack and Beth.

That was what he'd wanted, wasn't it? He'd wanted to scare her off. He should have felt nothing but relief that his plan had worked and his aunt's plotting hadn't succeeded, but he felt a little miffed, instead. That wasn't a good sign. All of the Carlton men loved a challenge.

Which probably meant that Destiny had advised Kathleen to go with her patented "always leave 'em wanting more" maxim. Alone with Destiny now, he gave his aunt a grim look.

"What are you up to?" he asked as she sat on the sofa, her feet tucked under her. With her soft cloud of brown hair and bright, clear brown eyes, she looked to be little more than a girl, though he knew perfectly well she was fifty-three.

Destiny sipped her brandy and regarded him without the slightest hint of guilt. "You're too suspicious, Ben. Why would I be up to anything?"

"Because it's what you do. You meddle. Ever since you decided Richard, Mack and I were old enough to settle down, you've systematically worked to make it happen."

"Of course I have. I love you. What's wrong with wanting to see you happy?"

"I am happy."

"You're alone. Ever since Graciela died, you've been terribly unhappy and guilt-ridden. It's time to put that behind you, Ben. What happened was not your fault."

"I'm not discussing Graciela," he said tightly.

"That's the problem," Destiny said, undaunted for once by his refusal to talk about what had happened. "You've never talked about her, and I think perhaps it's time you did. She wasn't the paragon of virtue you've built her up to be, Ben. That much has to be clear, even to you."

"Destiny, don't go there," Ben warned. He knew that his family had never held a high opinion of Graciela, but he'd refused to listen then, and he was equally adamant about not listening now, even with all of the facts still burning a graphic image in his head. He'd seen her with that polo player, dammit. He didn't need to be reminded of what were only rumors and speculation to everyone else.

"I will go there," Destiny said fiercely. "She was hardly a saint."

"Dammit, Destiny—"

She cut him off with a look that made her disapproval of his language plain. "Leaving her was the right thing to do, Ben. You're not responsible that she stormed off that night far too upset and drunk to be driving, and crashed her car into a tree. That was her doing, *hers*," she repeated emphatically. "Not yours."

Ben felt the words slamming into him, carrying him back to a place he didn't want to go, to a night he would never forget.

The argument had been heated, far more volatile than any that had gone before. He'd caught Graciela cheating on him that afternoon, found her with a neighboring Brazilian polo player, but she'd tried to explain away what he'd seen as if there could possibly be an innocent explanation.

In the past he would have accepted the lies, because it was easier, but he'd reached the end of his rope.

Loving her and forgiving her had worn him down, the cycle unending despite all the promises that she would change, that she would be faithful. He'd been foolish enough to believe them at first. He had loved her unconditionally and for a time had thought that accepting her flaws was a part of that.

Then he'd realized that what he felt wasn't love, but an obsessive need not to lose someone important again. He'd seen the truth with blinding clarity that afternoon. He'd realized finally that he'd never really had her anyway.

On that fateful night he'd told her to get out and he'd meant it. Her hold on him had finally snapped.

"You'll change your mind," she'd said confidently, slurring her words, her expression smug, beautiful even in her drunken state.

"Not this time," he'd told her coldly. "It's over, Graciela. I've had enough."

If that had been it, he could have moved on with his life, buried the repeated humiliations in the past and kept his heart hopeful that someone else would come along. But Graciela hadn't even made it out to the main highway when she'd crashed. He'd heard that awful sound and run outside, only to find the mangled wreckage, her body broken and bloody and trapped inside as the first flames had licked toward the gasoline spilling across the drive.

Frantic, he'd tried to drag her to safety, knowing even as he struggled that it was too late, that nothing he could do would save her.

From that moment on, as the car exploded into a fiery inferno, Ben had shut down emotionally. It had stirred the images that had haunted him from childhood of his parents' plane going down into the side of a mountain on a foggy night. He'd been so young back then that he'd barely understood what had happened. Everyone was careful to tiptoe around the details of that crash, so he'd filled in the blanks for himself, envisioning the kind of unbearable horrors that only a child with an active imagination could spin.

Now he shuddered and tried to push from his mind all of those memories, forever intertwined even though they'd occurred years apart.

"There's a huge difference between being alone and being lonely," he pointed out quietly. "No one should recognize that better than you. I don't see you trying to snag a husband now that your nest is empty, Destiny."

She frowned at the challenge. "It doesn't mean I wouldn't like to have companionship if the right man came along."

"There," he said triumphantly. "The *right* man, and nothing less."

"Well, of course." She gave him a sad smile. "I had that extraordinary experience once. I know what it's like. I won't accept anything less."

"Neither will I."

"But you won't find it, if you don't get out and look," she scolded.

"So you've decided to bring the likely candidate to my doorstep?"

She shrugged. "Sue me." Then she gave him a sly look. "It worked, didn't it? You're intrigued by Kathleen. I saw it in your eyes. You were watching her."

"Maybe I'd just like to paint her," he said, unwilling to admit to any more. Kathleen had been right, if Destiny knew about that kiss, he'd never hear the end of it. Who knew what she might do to capitalize on the impact of that kiss? Throwing them together at every opportunity would be the least of it.

Destiny chuckled. "You don't do portraits. If you are genuinely interested in painting her, I find that very telling, don't you?"

He refused to give her an inch. She would seize it and run with it for a mile. "Not particularly."

"Look at your choice of subjects, Benjamin," she said impatiently. "You're more comfortable with nature than you are with people. Ever since you lost your parents, you don't trust yourself to truly connect with anyone, much less to fall in love. Even Graciela was safe, because she was incapable of real love. You knew that from the start, and it suited you. You're afraid we'll all leave you."

"I fell in love with Graciela," he insisted.

"I don't believe that for a minute, but let's say it's true. In the end, she only reinforced the pain," Destiny said.

They'd been through this before. Ben had copped to it, so he saw no need to belabor the point. "Yes," he said tersely.

"I haven't left. Richard and Mack haven't left. And you're beginning to let yourself care for their wives, too. They're here for the long haul. I'll wager that you'll lose your heart to the children when they come along, as well."

"More than likely," he agreed. Each time he felt Melanie's baby kick, it set off an odd tug of longing inside him. He envied his brother the joy that awaited him, no question about it.

"Then why not open yourself to the possibility that there might be someone special out there for you as well?"

"I don't need anyone," he declared flatly.

"We all need someone. If I haven't taught you that, then I've failed you miserably."

"*You* don't seem to need anyone."

"But I have memories," she said sadly. "Wonderful memories."

"And those keep you warm at night?"

"They bring me peace," she said. "Life is for living, darling. Never forget that."

"Unless fate steps in," he said. "Tricky thing, fate. You never quite know when it's going to bite you in the butt."

She sighed, her expression suddenly nostalgic. "No, you don't, do you?"

Ben seized on the rare hint of melancholy in her voice. "You're thinking about what you gave up to come and take care of us, aren't you?" he said.

"You say that as if I have regrets. It wasn't a sacrifice," she insisted, just as she had on so many past occasions. "I did what I had to do. You boys have brought nothing but joy into my life."

"But nothing to equal the man you left behind," he pressed, wishing for once she would share that part of her life. If he had his hang-ups, they were nothing next to the secrets that Destiny clung to and kept hidden from them.

"Water under the bridge," she insisted. "I have no regrets, and that's the point. People move forward, take risks, let people in. Holing up and protecting your heart doesn't keep you safe. It keeps you lonely." She gave him one of her trademark penetrating, steady looks. "I could give you Kathleen's phone number, if you like."

"I'm surprised you haven't had it tattooed to my hand while I slept."

"Tattoos are too tacky," she teased. "Besides, if I happen to be wrong just this once, I'd hate for you to have to explain it away the rest of your life."

Ben grinned despite his exasperation. "I love you, you know that, don't you?"

"Yes," she said, her expression totally serene. "And in the end you'll do what I expect. You always do."

Sadly, she had that right. He could call Kathleen Dugan in the morning or he could hold out against the inevitable. In the end, though, he would see her again. Kiss her again.

He just wanted to make sure it was on his own terms.

Chapter Four

By noon on Friday, Kathleen's gallery was packed with customers who'd read a review of Boris's work in the morning paper. As Destiny had expected, the critic had raved about his bold style and predicted great things. Collectors who'd left without buying or even expressing much interest at the opening were now eagerly lining up to pay the premium prices Kathleen had put on tags the instant she'd seen the review. At this rate, the show would be a sell-out before the end of the day.

Which meant she would have to find another artist for the schedule, she realized as an image of Ben's painting slipped into her head. It would be awfully convenient if she could talk him into an immediate showing, but the likelihood of that was somewhere between slim and none. Winning him over was going to take time, patience and persistence, something she didn't have at the moment.

She'd just written up her last sale of the morning and drawn a deep breath at the prospect of a midday lull, when Destiny breezed into the gallery, resplendent in a trim red coat with a fake-fur collar and a matching hat.

"Good morning, Kathleen," she said, her gaze going to the walls, where red Sold stickers were on more than half of the price tags. Her expression immediately brightened. "Didn't I tell you that a favorable review would turn the tide for Boris? The show is obviously a resounding success, after all."

"It is," Kathleen said happily. "Now if only I had something to replace it, once the buyers come back to claim their pieces. I've been able to hold most of them off for the next week, but after that these walls could be bare." She gave Destiny a sly look. "I don't suppose you'd like to help me out?"

"You saw for yourself how difficult Ben can be. I doubt you'll be able to talk him into a show quickly enough," Destiny said.

It was obvious to Kathleen that Destiny was deliberately misunderstanding her question. "I agree, but there is another Carlton artist who's quite good." She met Destiny's gaze evenly. "And I think she owes me one, don't you?"

Destiny returned her gaze without so much as a flicker of an eyelash. "Why on earth would I owe you anything, my dear?"

"You got me out to your nephew's house under false pretenses, didn't you?"

"False pretenses?" Destiny echoed blankly. "I don't understand."

The woman was good, no doubt about it. She almost sounded convincing, and she'd managed to look downright wounded.

"It was never about Ben's art, was it?" Kathleen pressed. "You simply wanted me to meet him."

"And now you have," Destiny said brightly, as if attaching no significance to that meeting besides the obvious contact with an artist. "I'm sure in time you can persuade him to let you sell his paintings."

"How do I know there are more paintings?" Kathleen asked. "I never got to see them."

Destiny didn't look a bit uncomfortable at that reminder. "Yes, well, the timing seemed to be a bit off, after all. Perhaps in a few days or a few weeks things will settle down a bit and you can go back out there. I'd recommend waiting until after the first of the year."

"Nearly six weeks? My, my. Ben must be mad as hell at your scheming," Kathleen guessed.

Destiny waved off the suggestion. "He'll get over it. Just give him a little time."

"Which I don't have. I need something new and exciting to promote before Christmas." She gave Destiny another piercing look. "A few pieces by Destiny Carlton would be a huge draw before the holidays. We could do a lovely reception."

"Absolutely not," Destiny said flatly. "I no longer show my work."

"Just like someone else in the family," Kathleen scoffed. "Why not? I know you're good, Destiny. You've let me see your paintings."

"Painting was something I did professionally years ago. Now I merely dabble."

"The way Ben claims to dabble?"

"Ben's a genius!" Destiny said fiercely. "Concentrate on winning him over, my dear, and forget about me.''

"Hard to do, when you're here and he's not.''

"He'll come around in time. In the meantime, I'm sure you'll find something wonderful for the gallery for the holiday season,'' Destiny said. "Even at the last second, there are dozens of local artists who'd be thrilled by an invitation to show their works here. Ask one of them. They'll accept. You're very persuasive, after all.''

Kathleen gave her a wry look. "I don't seem to be doing so well with you. Maybe all Carltons are immune to my charms.''

"Maybe you simply need to formulate a new strategy and try a little harder,'' Destiny advised. Her expression turned thoughtful. "My nephew has a sweet tooth. Since you bake all those delicious little pastries you serve at your events here, I'm sure you could use that skill to your advantage.''

Apparently satisfied that she'd planted her seed for the day, Destiny glanced at her watch and feigned shock. "Oh, dear, look at the time. I'm late. I just wanted to stop by and tell you how delighted I was to see that review and to tell you again that I'm so glad you were able to join us yesterday.''

"Thanks for including me,'' Kathleen said, giving up the battle of wits with Destiny for now. A retreat seemed in order, since it seemed unlikely she'd be able to change Destiny's mind.

"I really enjoyed meeting the rest of your family,'' she added with total sincerity, "Beth and Melanie especially. Chatting with them was very enlightening.''

Destiny gave her a sharp look. "Don't believe everything you're told, Kathleen.''

Kathleen chuckled at her worried expression. "Yes, I can see why you wouldn't want me taking their advice at face value."

"What did those two tell you?" she asked, clearly ready to defend herself against all charges.

"Nothing I hadn't already figured out for myself," Kathleen said. "You're a clever woman, Destiny. And a force to be reckoned with."

Destiny squared her shoulders. "I'll take that as a compliment," she said.

"I thought you might," Kathleen said, her grin spreading. "I'm not entirely convinced they meant it that way, though."

"Those two have nothing to complain about," Destiny grumbled. "If it weren't for me giving them and my nephews a timely nudge, their lives would be very different."

"I'm sure they would all concede that," Kathleen agreed. "But may I give you a piece of advice?"

"Of course."

"Don't count on getting your way where Ben and I are concerned."

Destiny looked amused. "Because you're made of tougher stuff?"

"Precisely."

"Darling, that only means you'll fall even faster and harder."

Abandoning Kathleen to ponder that, she swept out of the gallery, leaving only the scent of her expensive perfume and her warning to linger in the air.

Ben slapped a heavy layer of dark, swirling paint on the canvas and regarded it bleakly. It pretty much mirrored his mood ever since Thanksgiving. Anyone looking at the painting would see nothing but turmoil and confusion. Some fool critic would probably look at it and see evidence of madness, and maybe he had gone a little mad from the moment he'd met Kathleen Dugan. Heaven knew, he couldn't get her out of his head, which was something he hadn't expected.

Nor had he been able to paint, not with the delicate touch required to translate nature into art. The fiasco in front of him had started out to be a painting of Canada geese heading north, but he'd messed it up so badly, he'd simply started layering coats of paint over the disaster, swirling together colors simply to rid himself of the restless desire to be doing something artistic even when his talent seemed to have deserted him. Who knew? Maybe he'd discover a whole new style. Looking at the canvas, though, it didn't seem likely.

He was about to put a fresh canvas on the easel and start over when he heard the slam of a car door. He glanced outside and saw Mack climbing out of his SUV. He figured his big brother had probably come to gloat. One look at the painting in front of Ben and even without an ounce of artistic talent of his own, Mack would recognize that his brother was in a funk. To avoid that, Ben took the still-damp canvas and shoved it out of sight, then grabbed a blank one and sat it on the easel.

Mack came in seconds later, carrying a bag filled with sandwiches and bottles of soda. He glanced at the pristine canvas and raised an eyebrow.

"Artist's block?" he inquired, barely containing a grin.

"Nope," Ben lied. "Just thinking about a new painting. Haven't even picked up my brush yet."

Mack's gaze immediately went to the palette of paints that had clearly been in use recently. "Oh?"

"I finished something earlier," Ben claimed, knowing he was only digging the hole deeper. Mack might not know art, but he knew his brother. He was also pretty deft at recognizing an evasion when he heard one.

"Can I see?" he asked, his expression innocent. His eyes betrayed him, though. They were filled with amusement.

"No. I tossed it out," Ben claimed. "It wasn't coming together right."

"Maybe you were too close to it. Could be you'd lost perspective. I could give you my opinion," Mack offered cheerfully, clearly not buying the elaborate tale.

"I'd rather you just dole out one of those sandwiches and leave the art critiques to people who know what they're talking about," Ben groused.

"You mean people like Kathleen Dugan?" Mack asked, his expression perfectly bland as he handed over a roast beef sandwich. "She seems knowledgeable."

"It'll be a cold day in hell before I let her near my paintings," Ben retorted.

"Because you don't think she knows the business or because Destiny introduced you?" Mack asked, grinning broadly. "Can't say I blame you for not trusting our aunt's motivation in inviting Kathleen out here."

"Yeah, well, you would know, wouldn't you?" Ben said.

"That I would."

"Why are you here, by the way?"

"Just thought I'd drop by and see how you're doing," Mack claimed.

"You were here Thursday. It's only Saturday. How much could happen in a couple of days?"

"I'd say that depends on how sneaky Destiny is being," Mack said cheerfully. "Has Kathleen popped up yet?"

"No sign of her," Ben admitted.

Mack studied him intently. "Are you relieved about that?"

"Of course."

"You don't sound especially happy. Seemed to me the two of you hit it off okay the other night. Maybe you were hoping she'd turn up to pester you by now."

Ben gave him a sour look. "We were polite."

"Then that kiss was just a polite gesture?" Mack asked.

Ben felt his face burn. "What kiss?" he asked with what he thought was a pretty good display of complete ignorance. Surely Mack was just guessing, adding up one man, one woman, a bit of chemistry and drawing his own conclusion about what had happened while he'd been out of the room. Maybe he was simply drawing on the knowledge of what he would have done if left alone with an attractive woman, pre-Beth, of course.

"The kiss I stumbled across when I came back into the dining room," Mack replied, disproving Ben's theory. "Looked pretty friendly to me."

Faced with the truth, indignation seemed the only route left to him. "What the hell were you doing? Spying on us?" Ben demanded.

"Nope," his brother said, clearly undaunted. "Destiny sent me in to ask how many pies you wanted her to leave for you, so she'd know how many to give Beth and me to take to the hospital."

"I didn't hear you come in," Ben said defensively.

"Obviously."

Ben scowled at his brother. "You didn't race right back in the kitchen and report what you'd seen, did you?"

"Absolutely not," Mack said, his indignation far more genuine than Ben's. "I just told Destiny you said you'd had all the pie you needed and I should take the rest."

"*That's* why I couldn't find so much as a crumb when I went looking for a late-night snack," Ben grumbled.

Mack gave him an unrepentant smile. "I figured you owed me for not blabbing."

Ben sighed. "You're right. It's a small enough price to pay for not getting Destiny's hopes up. Who knows what she'd dream up, if she thought round one had gone her way."

"Oh, I don't think you're off the hook, little brother, not by any means. In fact, if I were you, I'd be looking over my shoulder from here on out. Something tells me you'll be seeing Kathleen every time you turn around."

Ben decided not to tell Mack that he was already seeing her everywhere. The blasted woman had crawled into his head and wouldn't leave.

When it came to business, Kathleen wasn't especially patient. The art world was competitive and she'd learned early to go after what she wanted before someone else snapped it up.

Though Destiny had suggested prudence where Ben was concerned, Kathleen decided not to take any chances. If, by some fluke, word about his talent leaked out, she could be competing with a crowd for the

chance to mount his first show, maybe even to represent his work. The fact that he intended to play hard-
to-get simply made the game more interesting.

She was back out in the rolling hills of Middleburg
by 7:00 a.m. on the Sunday after Thanksgiving. Leaves
on the trees were falling fast, but there were still plenty
of hints of the gold, red and burnished-bronze colors
of fall. On this surprisingly warm, sunny morning,
horses had been turned out to pasture behind white
fences. It was little wonder that Ben painted nature,
when he lived in a setting this spectacular.

Kathleen was armed for the occasion. She had two
extralarge lattes from Starbucks with her, along with
cranberry scones she'd baked the night before when
she couldn't get to sleep for thinking about Ben and
that stash of paintings his aunt had alluded to. She told
herself those scones were not bribery, that she hadn't
taken Destiny's advice about Ben's sweet tooth to
heart. Rather they were simply a peace offering for
intruding on his Sunday morning.

She was waiting in her car with the motor running
when Ben emerged from the house, wearing yet another pair of disreputable jeans, a sweatshirt and sneak-
ers. Unshaven, his hair shining but disheveled, he
looked sexy as hell. All dressed up, he would be devastating.

But she wasn't here because Ben sent her hormones
into high gear. She was here because his talent gave
her goose bumps. Sometimes it was hard to separate
the two reactions, but in general she steered clear of
artists in her personal life. Most were too self-absorbed,
the emotional ride too bumpy. If that was her basic
philosophy, avoiding the dark, brooding types was her

hard-and-fast rule, learned by bitter experience. Ben Carlton was off-limits to her heart. Period.

Seemingly, though, her heart hadn't quite gotten the message. It was doing little hops, skips and jumps at the sight of him.

She expected a quick dismissal and was prepared to argue. She wasn't prepared for the hopeful gleam in his eye the instant he spotted the coffee.

"If one of those is for me, I will forgive you for showing up here uninvited," he said, already reaching for a cup.

"If the coffee gets me inside your studio, what will these freshly baked scones get me?" She waved the bag under his nose.

"I'll call off the guard dogs," he said generously.

"There are no guard dogs," she said.

"You didn't see the sign posted at the gate?"

"I saw it. Your aunt told me it was for show."

"No wonder people come parading in here whenever they feel like it," he grumbled. "I'll have to talk to her about giving away my security secrets."

"Either that or go out and buy a rottweiler," Kathleen suggested, taking the fact that he hadn't actually sent her packing as an invitation to follow him into the studio, which had been converted from a barn.

The exterior of the old barn wasn't much, just faded red paint on weathered boards, but inside was an artist's paradise of natural light and space. The smell of oil paint and turpentine was faint, thanks to windows that had been left cracked open overnight. Ben moved methodically around the room to close them, then switched on a thermostat. Soon warm air was taking away the chill.

Kathleen had to stop herself from dumping everything in her hands and racing straight to the built-in racks that held literally hundreds of canvases. Instead, she bit back her impatience and set the bag of scones on the counter directly in front of Ben.

"All yours," she told him.

Apparently he was the kind of man who believed in savoring pleasure. He opened the bag slowly, sniffed deeply, then sighed. "You actually baked these?"

"With my own two hands," she confirmed.

"Is this something you do every Sunday, get a sudden urge to bake?"

"Actually this urge hit last night," she told him.

"Let's see if you're any good at it," he said as he retrieved one of the scones and broke off a bite. He put it in his mouth, then closed his eyes.

"Not bad," he said eventually, then gave her a sly look. "This will get you five minutes to look around. Promise to leave the bagful and you can stay for ten."

"There are a half-dozen scones in that bag. That ought to buy me a half hour at least," she bargained.

Ben regarded her suspiciously. "Are you here just to satisfy your curiosity?"

Kathleen hesitated on her way to the first stack of paintings that had caught her eye. She had a feeling if she told him the truth, he'd hustle her out the door before she got her first glimpse of those tantalizingly close canvases. If she lied, though, it would destroy whatever fragile trust she was going to need to get him to agree to do a show.

"Nope," she said at last. "Though what art dealer wouldn't be curious about a treasure trove of paintings?"

"Then you still have some crazy idea about getting me to do a showing at your gallery?"

Kathleen shrugged. "Perhaps, if your work is actually any good."

He frowned. "I don't care if you think I'm better than Monet, I'm not doing a show. And your ten minutes is ticking by while we argue."

She smiled at his fierce expression. "We'll see."

"It's not going to happen," he repeated. "So if that's your only interest, you're wasting your time."

"Discovering an incredible talent is never a waste of my time."

"In this case it is, at least if you expect to make money by showing or selling my paintings."

She walked back to the counter where he sat, now crumbling one of those scones into crumbs. "Why are you so vehemently opposed to letting others see your work, Ben?"

"Because I paint for the joy it brings me, period."

She gave him a penetrating look. "In other words, it's too personal, too revealing."

Though he quickly turned away, Kathleen saw the startled look in his eyes and knew she'd hit on the truth. Ben put too much of himself into his paintings, he exposed raw emotions he didn't want anyone else to guess at.

"Bottom line, it's not for sale," he said gruffly. "And your time has just run out. I can live without the scones. Take the rest and go."

Kathleen cast a longing look in the direction of the paintings she had yet to glimpse, but she recognized a brick wall when she ran into it. Maybe Destiny had been right, after all, and she should have waited longer before coming back out here. Ben's defenses were solid and impenetrable at the moment.

"Okay then," she said, resigned. "I'll go, but I'll

leave the scones.'' She walked around until she could look him directly in the eyes. ''And I'll be back to claim that half hour tour you promised me.''

''It was ten minutes, but don't bother. You'll be wasting your time,'' he said again.

''My choice,'' she said pleasantly. ''And fair warning, you have no idea how persuasive I can be when I put my mind to it. This morning was just a little warm-up.''

Her gaze clashed with his and it gave her some satisfaction that he was the first to look away.

''I think maybe I'm getting the picture,'' he muttered.

Kathleen had heard him perfectly clearly, but she feigned otherwise. ''What was that?''

''Not a thing, Ms. Dugan. I didn't say a thing.''

''It's Kathleen,'' she reminded him.

This time he caught her gaze and held it. ''It's Kathleen if this thing between us is personal,'' he told her. ''As long as you think it's business, it's Ms. Dugan.''

There was another hint of challenge in his low voice. Since she knew he wasn't looking for a relationship any more than she was, it had to be deliberate. A scare tactic, basically. Just like that kiss on Thanksgiving.

She kept her own gaze steady and unblinking. ''Then by all means, let's make it Kathleen,'' she taunted, throwing down her own gauntlet.

Surprise lit his eyes. ''Obviously you've forgotten about that kiss we shared or you wouldn't be quite so quick to tempt me.''

Kathleen trembled. Her blood turned hot. That kiss hadn't been out of her mind for more than a minute at a time for the past couple of nights. What the hell had she been thinking by throwing out a dare of her own?

She should be concentrating on getting those pictures of his, not on reminding him of the chemistry between them.

"You don't scare me," she said with sheer bravado.

"I should."

"Why is that?"

"Because even though I'm sadly out of practice, when I want something—*someone*—I usually get exactly what I go after," he told her, his gaze steady and unflinching.

He made it sound like fact, not arrogance, which should have terrified her, but instead merely made her knees weak.

"You still don't scare me," she repeated, half expecting—half hoping—for a wicked, dangerous kiss that would immediately prove her wrong.

As if he'd guessed what was in her head, he backed away a step and shoved his hands in his pockets. "Stay away, Kathleen."

"I can't do that."

"Please."

She should do as he asked. There was no question about that. It would be smart. It would be safe. If it weren't for the art, maybe she could.

If it weren't for the man with the torment burning in his eyes, maybe she would.

As it was, there wasn't a chance in hell she'd do the smart, safe thing.

Chapter Five

"It's Sunday. Where on earth have you been? Not at that little shop of yours, I hope," Prudence Dugan said the minute Kathleen picked up her phone.

It was typical of her mother that she could manage to inject so much criticism, petulance and disdain into so few words. Kathleen wasn't in the mood to be drawn into an argument. All she really wanted to do was take a long, hot bath and think about the quicksand she was playing in with Ben Carlton.

"Did you call for any particular reason, Mother?"

"Well, that's a fine greeting," her mother huffed, oblivious to the fact that her own greeting had been less than cheerful. "When I didn't hear a word from you on Thanksgiving, I was worried."

Kathleen bit back the impatient retort that was on the tip of her tongue. She knew perfectly well this wasn't about any sudden burst of maternal concern. If it had been, her mother would have called on Friday or even Saturday.

No, the truth was that Prudence was incapable of thinking of anyone other than herself. She always had been. No matter how bad things had gotten with Kathleen's father or the succession of stepfathers that had followed, Kathleen had always been told not to rock the boat. Silence was as ingrained in her as were proper table manners. Her mother had never seemed to notice the high price Kathleen had paid for living up to her mother's expectations.

"Did you have a nice Thanksgiving, Mother?" she asked, because it was obviously what her mother expected.

"It would have been lovely if I hadn't had to spend the entire meal making excuses for you."

"You didn't need to make excuses for me. I'm perfectly capable of making my own."

"But that's the point," Prudence said irritably. "You weren't here, were you? Your grandfather was not pleased about that."

The only person in Kathleen's life who was stiffer and more unyielding than her mother was Dexter Dugan, patriarch of the Dugan clan. Yet somehow he'd managed to turn a blind eye to his daughter's foibles. He'd even encouraged Prudence and Kathleen to take back the prestigious Dugan name, no matter how many men had followed in Kathleen's father's footsteps. It was that blend of love and restraint that had confused her early on.

Once, Kathleen had tried to tell him about what was going on at home. She'd run to him crying, choking out the horror of watching her father hit her mother, but before the first words had left her mouth, her grandfather had shushed her and said she was never to speak of such things again. He'd told her she was far too young to understand what went on between adults.

"More important, what happens inside this family is never to be shared with outsiders," he told her sharply. "Whatever you see or hear is not to be repeated."

The comment had only confused her. He was family, not an outsider. She'd only been able to conclude that there was to be no help from him for the violence at home.

Despite her grandfather's admonishment, though, her father had suddenly left a few days later. Kathleen had wanted desperately to believe that her grandfather had relented and dealt with the situation, but she'd never quite been sure, especially when the pattern between her mother and father had been repeated over and over with other men. Kathleen never spoke of it again, but the men always left eventually, usually after some particularly nasty scene, so perhaps her mother was the one who eventually stood up for herself.

Only as an adult had Kathleen recognized that her mother would always be a victim, that she saw herself that way and sought out men who would see that nothing changed in that self-perception. Perhaps it was the only way Prudence could justify turning to her parents for the financial stability that her marriages never provided.

Whatever the reason, the cycle had been devastating for Kathleen, giving her a jaundiced view of relationships. Her grandfather's seemingly accepting attitude had reinforced that view. When her own marriage had crashed against the same rocks, she'd put an immediate end to it and vowed never to take another chance. Obviously, Dugan women were prone to making lousy, untrustworthy choices when it came to men. She, at least, was determined not to be a victim.

"I spoke to Grandfather and Grandmother myself Thanksgiving morning," Kathleen told her mother now. "If he was hassling you about my absence, I'm sorry. I thought I'd taken care of that."

Her mother sniffed. "Yes, well, you know how he can be."

"Yes, I do," Kathleen said dryly. They were two of a kind, grand masters of employing guilt as a weapon.

"What did you do on the holiday?" Prudence asked, now that she'd been somewhat mollified. "You didn't work, I hope."

"No. I was invited to have dinner with friends."

"Anyone I might know?"

"I doubt it. Destiny Carlton invited me. She's been a good friend to me and to my gallery."

"Carlton? Carlton?" Her mother repeated the name as if she were scrolling through a mental Rolodex. "Is she part of the family that owns Carlton Industries?"

"Yes, as a matter of fact. Her nephew Richard is the CEO. I'm surprised you've heard of the company."

"Your grandfather has some dealings with them," her mother said, proving that she wasn't entirely oblivious to the family's business holdings even though she'd never worked a day in her life. "Richard would be quite a catch. He's about your age, isn't he?"

"He's a bit older, but he's also happily married and expecting his first child," Kathleen replied with a hint of amusement. "I think you can forget about that one, Mother."

"Isn't there another son?" Prudence asked hopefully. "He owns some sports franchise, a football team or something like that, perhaps."

"That's Mack. Also married."

"Oh." Her mother was clearly disappointed. "Why would Destiny Carlton invite you over if there are no available men in the family?"

Kathleen wasn't surprised her mother didn't know about Ben. Not only did he stay out of the public eye, but he was an artist, a career not worthy of note in her mother's book. That was one reason she dismissed Kathleen's gallery as little more than a ridiculous hobby. If she'd seen the profits, she might have taken a different attitude, but it was doubtful.

"I'm fairly certain Destiny invited me because she thought I'd enjoy spending the day with her family," Kathleen responded, deciding not to mention Ben.

"And spending the day with strangers is preferable to being at home with your own family, I suppose," her mother said, the petulance back in her voice.

Kathleen lost patience. "Mother, that was not the issue. I stayed here because I wanted to work Friday and Saturday. I'd already made that decision and spoken to you by the time Destiny said anything at all about joining them. When she found out I had no plans, she included me in hers. I think it was very generous of her."

"Of course, your *work* was what actually kept you away," her mother said scathingly, making it sound like a dirty word. "How could I have forgotten about that?"

Kathleen desperately wanted to tell her mother that perhaps if she'd had work she loved, she might not have fallen into so many awful relationships, but again she bit her tongue. Getting into an argument wouldn't serve any purpose. They'd been over the same ground too many times to count, and it never changed anything.

"Mother, why don't you come down to visit and see the gallery for yourself?" she asked, knowing even as she made the invitation that she was wasting her breath. Her mother hadn't made the trip even once since Kathleen had opened the doors. Seeing her daughter happy and successful didn't fit with her own view of a woman's world. Kathleen had finally come to accept that, too, but she kept trying just the same. Maybe if her mother met someone like Destiny, it would enlighten her, as well. Heaven knew, Kathleen's grandmother with her passive nature hadn't been an especially good role model.

"Perhaps one of these days I'll surprise you," her mother said.

There was an oddly wistful note in her voice that Kathleen had never heard before. She took heart. "I hope you will," she said quietly. "I really mean that, Mother."

"I know you do," her mother said, sounding even sadder. "I am glad you had a nice holiday, Kathleen. I really am."

"I wish yours had been happier," she told her mother.

"My life is what it is. Take care, dear. I'll speak to you soon."

She was gone before Kathleen could even say goodbye. Slowly she hung up the phone and felt the salty sting of tears in her eyes, not for herself, but for the woman whose life had been such a bitter disappointment. Kathleen wanted to shout at her that it wasn't too late, but who was she to say that? Maybe for her mother who'd allowed herself to be defeated at every turn, it was impossible to imagine that there was any hope to be had, much less reach out for it.

"Let that be a lesson to you," Kathleen muttered to herself, immediately thinking of Ben.

That was the difference between herself and her mother, she told herself staunchly. She wasn't going to let any man defeat her. She'd get those paintings of his and maybe even a few more of those amazing kisses. She just had to be careful she didn't lose her heart along the way.

Ben gave up any attempt at painting after Kathleen left on Sunday. If his feeble attempts on Saturday had been a disaster, anything he tried after seeing her again was bound to be worse. The fact that she was affecting his work irritated the daylights out of him, but he was a realist. When the muse was in turmoil, he might as well get away from the farm.

Going to see his family was completely out of the question. His unexpected arrival on any of their doorsteps would be welcomed, but it would also stir up a hornet's nest of questions he didn't want to answer. Mack was out of town with the team, anyway, and Richard was probably driving Melanie mad with his doting. As for Destiny, her home was absolutely the last place he could turn up.

Usually he would have been content with his own company, maybe a good book, a warm fire and some music, but he knew instinctively that none of that would soothe him today.

Maybe he'd go for a drive, stop in one of the restaurants in his old neighborhood and have a good meal. If that put him in proximity to Kathleen's art gallery and gave him a chance to peek in the windows, well, that was nothing more than coincidence. Happenstance. Accidental.

Sure, and pigs flew, he thought darkly.

Still, once he was on the road, he headed unerringly toward Alexandria, cursing all the way at the traffic that didn't even take a rest on Sundays anymore. What the hell was wrong with all these people, anyway? Surely they couldn't all be suffering from the same sort of malaise that had gotten him out of the house. Wasn't anybody content with their lives, anymore? Did everyone have to go shopping? He directed the last at the lineup of cars backed up in the turn lane to a mall.

By comparison, Old Town Alexandria was relatively quiet and peaceful. There were still cobblestone sidewalks here and there and an abundance of charm. The big chain stores hadn't made many inroads here. He parked off King Street and got out to walk. If he stayed away from the street where the family town house was, there was little chance he'd run into his aunt.

Destiny was probably sitting in front of a fire with her feet tucked under her, a glass of wine at her side and some sort of needlework in hand. She'd recently taken up—and quit—crocheting and knitting. He suspected her attempts at cross-stitching wouldn't last, either. Once she'd tried quilting and given up on that, he figured she might be ready to do some serious painting again. It was obvious to him that these other creative outlets were no match for the talent God had given her.

Ben turned a corner on a street near the Potomac River and stopped short. There it was right in front of him, Kathleen's gallery. The bold, modern paintings in the window weren't to his taste, but he could appreciate the technique and the use of color. He wondered what had drawn Kathleen to them. Was it the art or the artist?

A black-and-white photo of the man had been blown up, along with a brief biography, and placed on an easel between the two paintings. The man wasn't handsome in the conventional sense. His expression was too fierce, his eyes too close-set. Shifty looking, Ben concluded. He scowled at the portrait, feeling a startling streak of jealousy slice through him.

Maybe if it hadn't been for that, he would have ignored the light that was on in the back of the shop. Maybe he would have done the smart thing and crept away before getting caught lurking around outside Kathleen's gallery like some lovesick kid.

Instead, he walked over to the door, tried it, then pounded on the door frame hard enough to rattle the glass panels.

When Kathleen emerged from the back, she looked as if she were mad enough to spit. Ben didn't care. He wasn't particularly happy himself.

"What are you doing here?" she demanded as she jerked open the door. "I'm closed."

"I thought you were anxious for me to see the place," he said, shoving his hands in his pockets and avoiding her gaze. The impulse to drag her into his arms was almost impossible to resist. He wanted to feel her mouth under his again, wanted to taste her. Instead, he resorted to temper. "I can see that I came at a bad time, though. Forget it."

He turned to go, only to hear her mutter an oath he wouldn't have expected to cross such perfect lips. Oddly, it made him smile.

"Don't go," she said eventually. "You just caught me in a particularly foul mood. I wouldn't even be here, except I was afraid if I stayed at home I'd start breaking things.''

He turned back slowly. ''Who put you in such a temper?'' he asked curiously. ''Or was it left over from our encounter this morning?''

''You merely exasperated me. My mother's the only person who can infuriate me.''

''Ah, I see,'' Ben said, though he didn't. His own family relationships were complex, but rarely drove him to the kind of rage Kathleen had obviously been feeling before his arrival. He met her gaze. ''Want to get out of here before you start slicing up the paintings?''

She gave him a hard look. ''I thought you came to see the paintings.''

''So did I, but apparently I came to see you,'' he admitted candidly. ''Have you had dinner?''

''No. I figured food and all that acid churning in my stomach would be a bad combination.''

''As a rule, you'd probably be right, but I think we can deal with that.''

She regarded him curiously. ''How?''

''We'll take a long walk and release all those happy endorphins. By the time we eat, you'll be in a much more pleasant frame of mind.''

''Unless you exasperate me,'' she suggested, but there was a faint hint of amusement in her eyes.

''I'll try not to do that,'' he assured her seriously.

''Then dinner sounds good. I'll turn off the lights and get my coat. I'll just be a minute.'' She hesitated, her gaze on him. ''Unless you really do want to look around.''

''Another time,'' Ben told her.

''Promise?''

He smiled and tucked a finger under her chin, rubbed his thumb across the soft skin. "Promise."

The word was out, the commitment made before he could remind himself that he never made promises, never committed to anything.

Ah, well, it was only a visit to an art gallery, he told himself. Where was the harm in committing to that?

He gazed into Kathleen's violet eyes and felt himself falling head-over-teakettle as Destiny might say. The shock of it left him thoroughly unsettled. If he'd been a lesser man, he'd have taken off the instant Kathleen went to get her coat, running like the emotional coward he was.

Instead he stayed firmly in place, telling himself there was no danger here unless he allowed it. No danger at all.

It was the first lie he'd told himself in years.

"Okay," Kathleen said as she sat across from Ben in a dark, candlelit restaurant that boasted some of the best seafood in town. "If we're going to get through dinner without arguing, here's what's off-limits—art, Destiny and my mother."

Ben lifted his beer in a toast. "Sounds perfectly reasonable to me." He gave her a disarming grin. "Think you can stick to it?"

"Me?" she scoffed. "You'll probably be the first to break the rules."

"Believe me, there was not a topic on your list that I'm interested in pursuing," he assured her. "If you want to talk about your favorite scone recipes, it's okay with me."

Kathleen grinned despite herself. "You want me to share my recipes with you?"

"Not share them," he said, giving her a look that made her toes curl. "I was thinking we could go to your place later and you could demonstrate."

"You got all the scones you're getting from me this morning," she assured him.

"Too bad. I'm really partial to the old-fashioned kind with currants. A dozen of those and I might let you have your way with me."

Now, there was an image meant to rattle her. She gave him a hard look meant to bring him back into line, then spoiled it by asking, "Are we talking sex or are we talking about me getting to poke around in your studio to my heart's content? No restrictions. No time limits."

"Which will be the best way to get you into the kitchen?"

"The studio, of course."

"Because?"

"Do you even have to ask? All that art just begging for an expert to appraise it."

He chuckled. "I win."

She stared at him blankly. "Win what?"

"You were the first one to break the rules and bring up art," he said.

She studied him with a narrowed gaze. "Then that entire discussion was some sort of game to get me to trip myself up?"

"Maybe."

"You're a very devious man."

"I come by it naturally."

"Destiny, I presume," she said, then groaned as she saw the trap. "Got me again."

He laughed. "Shall we move on?"

"To?"

He held her gaze and waited.

"I am not bringing up my mother, dammit!"

"Too late," he said, clearly delighted with himself. "And since you brought her up, tell me why she had you so upset that you had to leave home to save the crockery."

"The story is far too long and boring," she insisted, then smiled brightly. "And here's our food. Isn't that perfect timing?"

"Only if you think my memory is so short that I'll forget about this by dessert," he said mildly.

"I'm certainly counting on it," she told him.

For several minutes silence fell as they ate. Usually Kathleen was comfortable with silence. She rarely felt a need to fill it with inane chatter, but being with Ben was different. Maybe it was the fear that if she didn't initiate some innocuous topic, he would go right back to all the subjects that made her uncomfortable or caused conflict between them. She'd had all the conflict she could handle for one day. A quiet evening of pleasant conversation was what she wanted now. Ben was not the man she would have chosen for that, but he was here and, truthfully, they weren't doing so badly so far.

She glanced across the table and noted that Ben didn't seem to share the same fear that the silence would be filled with some disquieting topic. He seemed perfectly content to eat the excellent rockfish.

"Ben, what were you really doing in town this afternoon?" she asked eventually.

He looked vaguely startled by the question. "I told you. I came to see you."

"But you didn't know I'd be at the gallery," she said.

"No. And if I'm being perfectly honest, a part of me hoped that you wouldn't be."

"Why?"

He met her gaze. "Because seeing you only complicates things."

"How?"

"There's something between us, some powerful pull. That kiss the other night proved that." He paused and waited, apparently for some acknowledgment.

Hiding her surprise that he was willing to acknowledge that, Kathleen nodded.

"So we're agreed on that much," he said. "But unless I'm misreading the situation, you're not much happier about that than I am."

"Not much," she conceded.

"And you want something from me that I'm not prepared to give," he added.

"Your paintings."

"Yes. So, where does that leave us?"

She sighed at the complexity of the situation. He'd pegged it, all right. Then she brightened. "That doesn't mean we can't have a friendly meal together from time to time, does it? This is going pretty well so far."

He grinned. "So far," he said agreeably. "But what happens when I take you home and want to go inside and make love to you?"

Kathleen had just taken a sip of her tea and nearly choked on it. She stared at him. "Are you serious?"

"Very serious," he claimed, and there was nothing in his somber expression to suggest he was merely taunting her.

"Do you always want to sleep with someone you barely know?" she asked shakily.

"Never, as a matter of fact."

The fact that she was an exception rattled her even more than his initial declaration. But could she believe him? She didn't know him well enough to say if he was capable of a convenient lie or not. And Tim had been a smooth talker, too. Maybe it was some secondary gene in certain artists or maybe even in men in general. She reminded herself yet again that she needed to beware of anything that crossed Ben's lips, any admission that seemed to come too easily.

"I don't think it's going to be an issue," she said firmly, proud of the fact that she kept her voice perfectly steady. "Because the answer will be no."

"Because you don't want to?" he asked, his gaze searching hers. "Or because you do?"

"Doesn't really matter, does it? No is still no."

His lips quirked. "Unless it's maybe."

She frowned at that. "It most definitely isn't maybe."

He nodded slowly. "Okay then, friendly dinners are out because they could only lead to trouble. Any other ideas?"

Oddly, Kathleen desperately wanted to find a compromise. She was surprised by just how much she wanted to go on seeing Ben, whether he ever let her near his art or not. Not that she intended to give up on that, either.

"I'll give it some thought," she said eventually. "As soon as I come up with something, I'll let you know."

He gave her one of his most devastating smiles. "I'll look forward to that."

Still a little shaky from the impact of that smile, she studied him curiously. "Aren't you scared that your aunt will get wind of this and gloat or, worse yet, take it as a sign that her meddling is working and try a whole new plot?''

''Oh, I think we can count on Destiny getting mixed up in this again, no matter what we do,'' he said, sounding resigned. ''Unfortunately, she doesn't give up easily.''

He glanced up just then and groaned.

''What?'' Kathleen asked, then guessed, ''She's here, isn't she?''

''Just walked in,'' Ben confirmed. ''I imagine we can thank the maître d' for that. I swear the man is on her payroll. He probably called her the instant we came through the door.''

''Took her a while to get here, if he did.''

''She probably hoped to catch us in a compromising position,'' Ben said, then forced a smile as he stood up. ''Destiny.'' He gave her a kiss.

Kathleen gave her a weak smile. ''Nice to see you, Destiny.''

Destiny beamed at them. ''Please, don't let me interrupt. I just came in to pick up a dinner to take back to the house. I didn't feel much like cooking tonight.''

''Why don't you have them serve it here?'' Kathleen said. ''You can join us.''

Even as she spoke, Ben was saying, ''Don't let us hold you up. Your food will get cold.''

Destiny gave him a scolding look, then smiled happily at Kathleen. ''I'd love to join you, if you're sure you don't mind.''

Kathleen shot a fierce look at Ben. ''Please stay.''

Ben sighed heavily and relented. ''Have a seat,'' he said pulling out a chair for his aunt.

''Thank you, darling. I must say I'm surprised to see the two of you here together.''

"Surprised?" Ben asked skeptically. "I imagine you already knew we were here before you ever walked through the door. In fact, my guess is that it's what got you over here with that flimsy excuse about ordering takeout."

Destiny's gaze narrowed. "Are you suggesting I'm lying?"

"Just a little fib," he said. "You're not all that great at it, you know. You should give it up."

Destiny turned to Kathleen. "See what I have to put up with. I get no respect from this man."

"Oh, you get plenty of respect," Ben countered. "I'm just on to you."

Destiny sat back contentedly. "If you know why I'm here, that'll save me the trouble of asking all those pesky questions. Just tell me how you two wound up here."

"It was an accident," Ben claimed at once. "We bumped into each other."

"Alexandria is a long way from Middleburg. How did you just happen to be on the streets around here?" Destiny asked. "Were you coming to see me?"

"No," Ben said at once.

Destiny chuckled. "I see. Then it was the thought of seafood that drew you?"

"Something like that," Ben said.

Destiny regarded him smugly. "Something like that, indeed," she said, a note of satisfaction in her voice.

Kathleen stole a look at Ben. He did not look happy. In fact, judging from his expression, she figured their gooses were pretty much cooked. Destiny would never give up now.

Chapter Six

Ben spent two days kicking himself for choosing to take Kathleen to that particular restaurant for dinner. He knew perfectly well that Destiny had sources there. That was where Richard had met Melanie, and his aunt had had every detail of that meeting before they'd finished their first cups of coffee. Ben knew because she'd gloated about it.

Since he should have guessed the risks, did that mean some part of him had wanted to be caught? Was he hoping in some totally perverse way that Destiny would keep meddling until both he and Kathleen were firmly on the hook?

Surely not, especially after just a couple of brief encounters. He might be in lust with Kathleen, but it certainly didn't go beyond that, and beyond that is just where Destiny wanted him to go. He didn't believe for one single second that this was about art, not from his aunt's perspective, anyway.

But any relationship was doomed. He and Kathleen had discussed the situation and viewed it through clear eyes. It simply wasn't meant to be. Period.

That didn't mean he was having much success in ignoring the attraction. Goodness knows he was tempted to drag her into his arms about every ten seconds, but that was another thing they'd agreed on. Sex was a bad idea.

Not that they'd hold out forever, he concluded honestly, especially if they kept on seeing each other on one pretext or another. Proximity was about as dangerous for the two of them as holding a match near the wick on a stick of dynamite and simply hoping there wouldn't be an explosion.

He was still pondering the entire situation over his morning coffee when he looked up and spotted Richard coming up the front steps. First Mack, now Richard. His brothers were apparently determined to get an unprecedented amount of enjoyment out of watching him squirm.

Richard rang the bell, then used his key and came on in. No one in the whole damn family ever considered that he might be busy or might not want to see them, Ben thought gloomily. Maybe Middleburg hadn't been quite far enough to move when he'd wanted solitude. Ohio might have been better. Or maybe Montana.

"You in here?" Richard called out.

"If I weren't, would you go away?" Ben replied, not even trying to hide his sarcasm.

Richard strode into the dining room, picked up the

pot of coffee and poured himself a cup without bothering to respond.

"I'll take your silence as a no," Ben said. "If you're here to make something out of the fact that I had dinner with Kathleen, don't bother. I'm in no mood to discuss it."

Richard regarded him with seemingly genuine surprise. "You had dinner with Kathleen? When was that? You certainly didn't waste any time, did you? I thought you were made of tougher stuff than that."

"Very funny," Ben said, then frowned at his brother. "You mean Destiny didn't tell you? I thought she'd announce it to the wire services."

"Nope, and apparently she didn't see fit to tip off her favorite gossip columnist, either," Richard said with an exaggerated shudder. "Be grateful for small favors."

"I'm not feeling especially grateful," Ben told his big brother. "Okay then, let's change the subject. Why are you out here on a weekday morning, if not to gloat?"

"I needed a sounding board," Richard said.

His tone was so serious, his expression so gloomy, that Ben stared at him in shock.

"Is Melanie okay?" he asked at once. "There's nothing wrong with the baby, is there?"

"Aside from being annoyed with me for hovering, Melanie's perfectly fine. So is the baby," Richard said. "This is about business."

"And you came to me?" Ben asked, astonished. "Why not Mack? Or Destiny?"

"I didn't go to Mack because he's out of town," he admitted with typical candor. "And I didn't want to discuss this with Destiny, because the last time I brought up this particular subject, she got really weird on me.''

"Then I was third choice? That's a relief," Ben said. "I thought the business had to be close to collapse if you were desperate enough to seek advice from me."

"Actually, in this instance, you really were first choice. You know Destiny better than Mack or I do."

Ben groaned at the frequently-made claim. "That's ridiculous and you know it."

"Come on, Ben. It's no secret that the two of you are tighter than the rest of us. Maybe it's because you were the youngest when she came to live with us, so she was even more like a mother to you. Or maybe it's the art thing, but you're her favorite. I figure she's bound to share things with you that she doesn't confide in Mack or me."

"You've said something like that before, and I still say you're crazy," Ben said. "Destiny doesn't have favorites. Sure, we have a bond because of art, but that's it. She loves all of us."

"I know she loves us. That's not the point," Richard said impatiently. "Look, can we talk about this or not?"

Ben sat back. "Fine. Talk, but I have to tell you that Destiny does not sit around sharing confidences with me, either. She's meddling in *my* life these days. She's not letting me poke around in hers."

"That doesn't mean she hasn't let something slip from time to time," Richard insisted. "Here's the deal. I've got a huge problem with the European division. We've nearly lost out on a couple of big deals over there because of some minor player who jumps into the mix and drives up the price. So far we've only lost one acquisition, but that's one too many. And I don't like the fact that it's always this same guy whose name keeps popping up. It's like he's carrying out his own personal vendetta against Carlton Industries. This company of his is not a major player, but he's smart enough to know precisely what to do to make a muddle of our negotiations.''

Despite his total lack of interest in the family business, Ben hadn't been able to avoid absorbing some information over the years. Richard introduced the topic at almost every family gathering. Because of that, so far he was following Richard, but he didn't see the connection to their aunt.

''What does any of that have to do with Destiny?'' he asked.

''I'm not a hundred percent certain, but I think this was a man she was involved with years ago. It's the only explanation I can come up with,'' Richard told him.

''Have you asked her?''

''Of course. When I brought up his name, she turned pale and flatly refused to tell me anything. She said I was in charge of Carlton Industries and I should deal with it.''

The whole scenario seemed a little too far-fetched to Ben. Destiny with some long-lost secret love who'd been pining for years and was now making a move on Carlton Industries in retaliation for some slight? He'd always thought the business world was a whole lot more logical and, well, businesslike than that.

''What makes you think she knows him, much less was involved with him?'' he asked Richard. ''Maybe she simply doesn't want to get drawn into company politics.''

''I had someone in the division over there do some

quiet checking. I wanted to see if this man and Destiny could have crossed paths. The guy is British, but he lived in France for several years. In fact, he lived in the very town where Destiny lived at the same time she was there. That can't be pure coincidence. I even sent my guy over to France to poke around, but people wouldn't tell him a blessed thing. He said those who remembered her got very protective when he mentioned Destiny's name."

Ben had always known that Destiny had hidden things from them. Because of the vibrant, extraordinary woman she was, he'd also supposed that there had been a man in her life back then. Only recently had she alluded to such a thing, though. Even so, she hadn't acknowledged a broken heart and she certainly had never mentioned a name.

"I don't know, Richard," Ben said skeptically. "I suppose you could be right. It makes sense that there was someone in her life back then, but why would he be driven to make a play at this late date for companies Carlton Industries wants to acquire?"

"Beats me," Richard said candidly. "But I have this gut feeling there's a connection."

"Is he a real threat to the company?"

"More an annoyance," Richard admitted. "But I don't like anything I can't explain."

"Then you need to ask Destiny again."

"I thought maybe you could," Richard suggested, then grinned. "Since you're bound to be seeing more of her these days than I am, what with the whole Kathleen thing going on."

"Ha-ha," Ben retorted, unamused.

Richard's expression sobered at once. "Will you talk to her?"

"You really are worried, aren't you?" Ben asked.

"It's gnawing at me, yes. And there's a deal coming up soon that could be really important to our future growth in Europe. I don't want to have this particular gnat in the mix."

Ben nodded slowly. "Okay then, I'll do what I can, but you know how prickly Destiny is about the past. She's never wanted us to get the idea that she gave up anything important to come and take care of us. If she blew off your questions, she's just as likely to blow off mine."

"I think we're past the time when she needs to worry about us feeling insecure about her intentions toward us," Richard said. "We all know she loves us and that she has no regrets about the choice she made. I just need to know if she walked out on a love affair that could be coming back to haunt us."

"I'll see what I can find out. What's this man's name?"

"William Harcourt."

Ben pulled an ever-present pen out of his pocket and jotted the name down on his hand, since he didn't have paper handy and didn't trust his memory to even recall the conversation once he'd spent a few hours in his studio. Richard watched him, looking amused.

"Try not to wash up before you call Destiny," he advised.

Ben grinned. "Waterproof ink," he noted, waving the pen. "I learned that lesson a long time ago. I figure even with a few long, cold showers, I've got till the end of the week to remember to chase down Destiny and ask her about this."

"Don't wait that long, okay?"

Something in his brother's tone alerted him that this

mess was even more serious than Richard had admitted. Ben nodded.

"I'll get back to you tonight. Will that do?"

"Morning's soon enough," Richard assured him. "Tonight I have to wallpaper the nursery to keep Melanie from trying to do it herself."

Ben chuckled. "I'm sure she'll appreciate your consideration."

"Actually she won't," Richard conceded with a shrug. "She'll sit there and grumble and tell me I'm doing it all wrong."

"Then let her do it," Ben advised.

"Let her climb a ladder in her condition?" Richard asked with a look of genuine horror. "I don't think so. I can take three or four nonstop hours of grumbling."

"Do you even know how to hang wallpaper?" Ben asked curiously.

"No, but how hard can it be?"

Ben smothered a laugh. "I'll be by tonight."

"I told you morning's soon enough."

"Maybe for the report you want," Ben agreed. "I'm coming by for the entertainment."

She had no business going out to the farm, Kathleen told herself even as she turned onto the country road that led to Ben's. Destiny's arrival at the restaurant the other night had been fair warning that the meddling and matchmaking were far from over.

But she'd awakened this morning thinking about Ben—about his *art,* she corrected, determined to stay focused—and had decided that the only way she'd ever get what she wanted was to keep up the pressure. He'd had two days off now. As distracted as an artist could get, he could easily have forgotten all about her by now.

Before leaving the house, she'd taken an extra hour to bake some of the bear claws she made for the occasional morning receptions she held for the media to meet artists before their shows opened. She told herself she'd baked them because she'd had a sudden craving for one herself, but the truth was it was another bribe. If the man had a sweet tooth, she was not above exploiting it.

Just as she reached the end of Ben's driveway, she saw a car turning onto the main highway and recognized Richard behind the wheel. She waved at him as he passed and got a friendly wave and a smug grin in return.

Then she turned into the long drive leading up to the secluded house. Not that she was any expert on recluses, but it seemed to her that Ben's reputation for craving solitude was slightly exaggerated. In the few days she'd known him, he'd had plenty of company right here at the farm and he'd come into town to seek her out. That didn't sound like any recluse she'd ever heard about.

Still, there was no question that his expression was forbidding when he walked out of the house and spotted her just as she was pulling to a stop beside his studio.

"This place is turning into Grand Central Station," he complained.

Kathleen gave him a cheery smile. "I was just thinking the same thing. I saw your brother leaving."

Ben's scowl deepened. "Great. Just great. That will hit the family grapevine as soon as he can hit speed-dial on his cell phone."

"Still running scared of Destiny?"

"Aren't you?"

"Not so much. Besides, I'm here on business, not for pleasure."

"A distinction I'm sure Richard will make when he reports your arrival before eight in the morning."

She refused to be daunted. "At least he didn't catch me going in the other direction," she said. "Just imagine what he could have made of that."

Ben sighed, then glimpsed the bag in her hand. His expression brightened marginally. "Have you been baking again?"

"Bear claws," she told him. "I took a chance you'd like them."

"Real ones?" he asked incredulously. "With almond paste and flaky pastry? Fresh from the oven?"

She grinned at his undisguised enthusiasm. "As authentic as any bakery's."

He snatched the bag from her hand and peered inside, then drew in a deep, appreciative breath. "Oh, my God." He peered at her curiously. "Why aren't you married?"

"I was. He didn't seem to care that much for my baking."

"Fool."

Kathleen laughed. "He was, but not because he didn't like my pastry." It was the first time she'd ever been able to laugh at anything related to her marriage. She met Ben's gaze. "Since you're obviously awed and impressed, are these going to get me into your studio?"

His expression turned thoughtful as he took his first bite. "Fantastic," he murmured, still not answering her question.

He took another bite, then sighed with seeming rapture. "Incredible, but no."

Kathleen was tempted to snatch away the rest of the pastries. Instead, she settled for giving him a severe look. "May I ask why?"

He grinned. "You've made a slight miscalculation. Don't worry about it. People are always doing that where I'm concerned. They think I know very little about business, because I'm the artistic Carlton, but I did pick up a thing or two."

"So?"

"I've obviously got something you want, something you want desperately enough to ply me with baked goods. Why would I cave in too quickly, when holding out will get me more?"

Despite her frustration, Kathleen couldn't help chuckling. "You're impossible."

"So I've been told." He gave her a considering look. "But just so your trip won't be a total waste, how about going over to Richard and Melanie's with me tonight?"

Kathleen was startled by the invitation. "For?" she asked cautiously.

"We get to watch Richard try to hang wallpaper, while Melanie criticizes him."

Kathleen laughed. "Oh, hon, I think you're the one who's miscalculated. We set foot in there tonight and Richard won't be hanging that wallpaper alone. You'll be right in there with him, while Melanie and I sip tea in the kitchen."

"Want to bet?"

"Sure," she said at once, always eager to take advantage of an opportunity to best someone who'd just tricked her. "If it turns out the way I predict, you show me at least one more painting. If you win, I bring you the pastry of your choice next time I come.''

He considered the offer, then nodded. ''Deal. Oh, and just so you know, we have to take a little side trip past Destiny's on the way.''

''As in drive past and don't stop?'' she asked hopefully.

''Nope,'' he said, sounding oddly happy. ''We're dropping in to do a little snooping. I think it might require a woman's touch. What time does the shop close?''

''Five-thirty tonight.''

''Good. I'll pick you up at six.'' He looked her over. ''You might want to wear something you don't care too much about.''

''Oh?''

''If I wind up papering those walls, sweetheart, you won't be sipping tea. You'll be right there next to me.''

If he had a hundred years, Ben was pretty confident he wouldn't be able to explain what had made him ask Kathleen to join him in going to see Destiny. Oh, sure, maybe he'd had some vague notion that Destiny would be more inclined to open up to another woman, but it wasn't as if Kathleen were a trusted confidante. Melanie or Beth might have been better suited to the task.

No, he'd acted on impulse, something he never did, not since he'd been involved with Graciela, who'd taken impulsive behavior to an art form. Now he was usually thorough and methodical about just about everything, measuring words and actions, because he couldn't forget the last time he'd made an impulsive decision, demanded that Graciela leave his home immediately, and she had died because of it.

But despite his misgivings about the invitation to Kathleen for tonight, he hadn't called and canceled. It was yet another instance of making a commitment and then being too proud, if not too honorable or too stubborn, to break it. Kathleen already thought he was cowardly when it came to his art. He couldn't give her another reason to believe that he was scared of her or his feelings for her.

He considered seeing Destiny first, then picking up Kathleen, but figured that would raise a whole lot of questions that he wouldn't want to answer, as well. Instead, he drove through the horrendous Washington rush hour traffic to the address Kathleen had given him. He was on her doorstep precisely at six. He reassured himself that it was absolutely not because he was anxious to see her again. He knew artists had a reputation for being forgetful, but punctuality was one of those lessons that had been ingrained in him by his parents even before Destiny had come along to reiterate it.

When Kathleen opened the door, his mouth gaped. He couldn't help it. She'd taken his advice to wear old, comfortable clothes to heart, but few women could turn that particular sort of getup into a fashion statement. Kathleen did. The faded, low-slung hip-hugger jeans encased her slender legs like a glove and reminded him all too vividly just how long those exquisite legs were. She was wearing a bulky knit sweater that looked warm enough, except for the full two inches of bare skin it left exposed at her waist.

"Um," he began, then swallowed hard. He cleared his throat and tried again. "Aren't you going to be cold?"

She grinned. "I was thinking of wearing a coat over this."

He nodded, still trying to get the blood that had rushed to other parts of his anatomy to flow back to his brain. "I meant indoors."

Her grin spread. "Your aunt doesn't have heat?"

Ben sighed and gave up. He wasn't going to get her into something that covered that enticing skin without point-blank asking her to change, and he would not do that. She'd only demand to know why, just to hear him admit that he could hardly keep his hands or his eyes off her. He'd simply have to suffer and keep a tight rein on his hormones.

"Let's get going, then."

Kathleen gave him a knowing smirk. "I'll get my coat," she said cheerfully.

On the drive to Destiny's, Ben finally managed to untangle his tongue long enough to explain their mission to get at the truth about Destiny and this William Harcourt who was interfering in Carlton Industries business.

"What makes you think I can get her to say anything, when Richard couldn't?"

"You're a woman. Maybe she'll confide in you, woman-to-woman."

"With you sitting there?"

"I'll make some excuse and hide out for a little bit," he said, no doubt sounding a little too eager.

Kathleen looked at him with amusement. "That will certainly make her less suspicious."

He had a hunch she was right. "Do you have a better suggestion?"

"Ask her directly. Even if she doesn't answer, you should be able to read her expression. And *I'll* be the one to make myself scarce while you do it. Women are always having to run to the powder room. She won't think a thing about it."

"I suppose," he said gloomily. He was no good at this kind of stuff. Subterfuge and subtlety weren't in his nature, but Richard had already warned him that the direct approach hadn't gotten him a thing.

"Trust me, Ben. It's the only way," Kathleen insisted. "A woman like your aunt appreciates someone who's straightforward. Trying to slip something past her won't work. Or if by chance it does, she'll be furious with you for having tricked her into saying something she didn't intend to reveal. That's the last thing you want."

"Okay, okay," he grumbled. "I know you're right. I just hate doing what I'm always accusing her of doing, meddling in something that's none of my business."

"Tell her that, too," Kathleen suggested. "She'll identify with your position. Heck, maybe it will even give her a nudge to back off with her own meddling."

"I think we can eliminate that possibility. I'm not in the miracle business," Ben responded.

He pulled up in front of the town house where he'd grown up. In some ways it still felt more like home than the farm, but at the moment he was dreading going inside. He glanced at Kathleen.

"I guess it's showtime," he said unenthusiastically.

"Don't sound like you expect to be shot on sight," she said, regarding him with obvious amusement. "This is Destiny. The mere fact that I'm with you ought to buy you a certain amount of good will."

It ought to, Ben agreed. But he had a hunch that Destiny was going to be more furious than smug tonight. He also had a gut feeling that he and Kathleen were going to be back out on the front steps in record time. In fact, given what Richard had told him earlier, there was a distinct possibility that Destiny might kick them straight to the curb.

Chapter Seven

Destiny's initial delight at finding Ben and Kathleen on her doorstep was pretty much doomed to fade quickly, quite likely because her nephew had absolutely no notion how to finesse such a touchy conversation. Kathleen barely contained a sigh when Ben declined a drink, declined to take off his coat. It was pretty much apparent that he was on a mission and he was impatient to get it over with. Kathleen spotted the immediate suspicion in Destiny's eyes at his curt manner.

"Actually we're on our way to Richard's," he told Destiny the instant they'd stepped inside. He showed absolutely no inclination to set one foot any farther into the house.

Destiny looked a bit taken aback, but quickly rallied. "Really? For dinner? And you invited Kathleen to join you. How lovely."

"We're probably going to order pizza," Ben told her, oblivious to the hopeful note in Destiny's voice. "Richard's wallpapering the nursery. And we're planning to watch."

Destiny's deep-throated chuckle cut through the tension. She seemed to relax a bit. "Yes, I can see how that would be immensely entertaining. Perhaps I'll come along."

"Sure," Ben said. "But I need to talk to you about something first." He glanced pointedly in Kathleen's direction.

"May I use the powder room, Destiny?" she asked dutifully.

Destiny clearly wasn't fooled for a second by the abrupt pretext. She gave Ben a piercing look. "What is this about?" When Kathleen started to leave, Destiny arrowed a look in her direction. "Stay right here, Kathleen."

"But—" Kathleen protested, only to be cut off.

"I would appreciate it if you would stay," Destiny repeated, then frowned at Ben. "Does this have anything at all to do with your brother or Carlton Industries?"

Ben stared at her in obvious shock. "How do you know that?"

"Oh, please, do you think I don't know what goes on over there?" Destiny scoffed. "I have an office right down the hall from your brother's. It might be mainly for window dressing, since I'm family and I am a member of the board, but I've been known to spend time there. I'm privy to what's going on in the company. I even have a secretary, as you very well know. And people actually stop in to chat from time to time.

There's very little that goes on around there that I don't know about.''

Kathleen bit back a smile as Ben sighed, and asked, ''More of your inside sources, I presume.''

''Of course,'' she said without apology. ''I know how invaluable contacts can be. It's how the business world works. And despite my refusal to take my proper place at Carlton Industries, it was impossible to grow up around your grandfather and father without learning a thing or two about how important it is to keep one ear to the ground at all times. It avoids a lot of nasty surprises.''

''Did your insider tell you what Richard is upset about?'' Ben asked.

''The European division,'' she said at once, proving that she didn't spend all of her time in that office sipping tea and gossiping with the friendly staff. ''It hasn't been performing as well as he'd hoped and he thinks it's being victimized by the owner of a British company.''

''Exactly,'' Ben said. ''A man named William Harcourt.''

Kathleen kept her gaze locked on Destiny's face when the name was mentioned. Aside from the faint shadow that darkened her eyes, she betrayed nothing.

''Do you know him, Destiny?'' Ben asked point-blank.

For a moment Kathleen thought Destiny was going to evade Ben's question. Instead she drew herself up regally.

''I did at one time,'' she admitted. ''But I imagine your brother already knows that. He certainly paid enough to that private detective who was poking around over there.''

Ben regarded her with chagrin. "You found out about that, too?"

"Darling, I lived in that village in France for a number of years. Of course I have friends there who would let me know about a stranger who was asking too many questions. It wasn't all that difficult to find the payments to him on the Carlton Industries books."

Kathleen was impressed. "Nice work, Destiny."

Ben shot a daunting look at both of them. "Let's cut to the chase, then. How well do you know William Harcourt?" he asked bluntly.

"The answer to that depends on many factors," Destiny said evasively.

Ben gave her an impatient look. "It's not a difficult question, Destiny. Any answer at all will do, as long as it's truthful."

She frowned at his tone. "I don't see the need to discuss this with you."

"Then you'll just have to discuss it with Richard," he warned.

"Oh, for heaven's sakes, the two of you are acting as if there's some grand conspiracy. I haven't seen William or heard from him in years."

"Did you know him well?" Ben asked again, this time more gently, as if he'd finally caught on to just how touchy this subject was.

"I really don't think that matters," Destiny said stiffly.

"It does if you're the reason he's targeting Carlton Industries," Ben said.

"That's absurd," Destiny said flatly. "Tell your brother that whatever's going on has nothing to do with me. I'm certain of that. If he's found himself in a hostile business environment over there, he needs to fix the problem. Richard is the one in charge, after all. I'm sure William will be reasonable."

"Why don't you tell Richard that yourself?" Ben asked. "You two can talk this out when we get to his house. Given your insights, maybe you can give Richard some advice on how to handle the man."

Destiny shook her head, looking suddenly tired. "I don't think I'll go after all. I've just remembered a prior engagement."

"Destiny—"

Kathleen cut off Ben's protest, even as she gave Destiny's icy hand a squeeze. "It's okay, Ben. We should be going."

Ben looked as if he might argue, but Kathleen all but shoved him toward the front door. Only after he was outside did she claim to have forgotten her purse.

"Start the car. I'll be right with you," she told him.

He gave her a penetrating look. "What are you up to?"

"I'm not up to anything," she insisted.

He studied her with obvious skepticism, then shrugged. "Okay, whatever. I'll warm up the car."

Kathleen hurried back inside and found Destiny still standing where they'd left her. "Are you okay? Is there anything I can do for you?"

Destiny tried to smile, but failed. "No, dear, there's nothing anyone can do."

"This Mr. Harcourt really mattered to you, didn't he?"

Destiny's expression turned even sadder. "He was the love of my life," she said simply, her voice catching.

"But none of your nephews knows that, do they?"

"No, I never saw the point in telling them. It ended when I came back to the States to care for them."

"Maybe it's time you explained all that."

Destiny shook her head. "I've never wanted them to think there was any sacrifice at all in my returning home to look out for them. It would only have upset them. Besides, it's in the past."

"It doesn't sound as if Mr. Harcourt agrees with you," Kathleen pointed out.

Destiny looked startled by that. "What on earth are you saying?"

"That Ben could be correct. You could be the reason Mr. Harcourt has become a thorn in Richard's side. Sooner or later you'll have to consider that and deal with it."

Destiny sighed heavily. "Perhaps you're right," she said slowly.

"And if I am?"

A glint of determination suddenly lit Destiny's eyes and she squared her shoulders, looking stronger than she had since the whole topic had come up. "Then I will deal with William," she said firmly.

Kathleen grinned at her fierce tone. "If you need any help, let me know."

"Thanks for helping me to clarify what I must do," Destiny said. "But if you wouldn't mind, please keep this conversation to yourself. Until I decide how I want to handle this, it's best that Ben and the others don't know about my intentions."

"They could help," Kathleen suggested, uncomfortable at being asked to keep Destiny's secret from Ben. He wasn't going to be happy if she left the house tonight without something to report.

Destiny laughed. "I love my nephews, Kathleen, but

in a situation like this, they won't help. They'll only pester me to death.''

"The way you meddle in their lives?"

"Exactly." Destiny gave her a wry look. "I did raise them, after all."

Ben was thoroughly frustrated. Kathleen had refused to reveal a single word about her conversation with Destiny.

"Confidential," she said when he asked.

"But I'm the one who wanted you to talk to her," he protested.

"And I told you to handle it yourself. Just look how well that turned out. She clammed up and refused to reveal a single thing about her knowledge of this Harcourt person."

"She admitted she knew him," Ben said defensively.

"Oh, please," she scoffed. "You knew that before you ever walked in there. So did Richard, I suspect. What you knew nothing about was the extent of the relationship and how it fits with what's going on now. You don't know any more about that than you did before you spoke to her."

He regarded her intently. "Do you?"

"Confidential," she said again.

"I'll bet Richard can pry it out of you," he said.

"Doubtful," she said.

"Or Melanie," he suggested.

She chuckled. "I don't think so. Whatever Destiny did—or didn't say—to me is not going to cross these lips. Give it up, Ben."

"I might reconsider letting you see a few paintings," he coaxed.

"We already have a bet going that I plan on winning. I'll see at least one of the paintings as soon as you wind up wallpapering that nursery right alongside Richard." She gave him a sideways look. "Unless you intend to renege on our deal."

"Not a chance."

She regarded him with a cheerful expression. "Any other offers you want to put on the table?"

"Not at the moment," he said, exasperated. "I'll get back to you."

"Yes, I imagine you will." Her smile expanded. "It's nice to know that I now have something *you* want. Sort of evens the playing field, doesn't it?"

"You're a sneaky woman. You know that, don't you?"

"Of course."

"It must be why Destiny has taken to you."

"That's one reason," Kathleen agreed. "The other has a lot to do with this impossible nephew she's trying to marry off."

Ben was surprised that she could joke about that. "I thought you found that idea as terrifying as I do."

"Maybe it's growing on me."

He stared at her in shock. "You have to be kidding me."

Kathleen laughed at the unmistakable panic he didn't bother trying to hide. She reached over and patted his white-knuckled grip on the steering wheel. "No need to panic. As flattering as it is to be considered a candidate to be your wife, I'm not interested."

There was no question that she meant exactly what she said. Ben should have been comforted by that, but for some reason he didn't understand, he felt as if someone had just doused him with cold water.

* * *

"Well, don't you two look cheery," Richard said as Ben and Kathleen arrived a few minutes later.

"You don't look so hot yourself," Ben retorted, shocked to see his usually impeccable brother covered with some sort of white paste. His hair was a mess and his expression was grim. "Things not going too well?"

"Don't start with me," Richard warned. "Otherwise you can take your sorry ass out of here right now." He turned to Kathleen. "No offense."

"None taken," she said, her lips twitching as she fought a grin.

"Fine," Ben said, holding up his hands in a gesture of surrender. "I'll keep my comments to myself. Where's Melanie?"

"Actually she's in the nursery with her feet propped up, a glass of milk beside her and a gloating expression on her face. She's having the time of her life," Richard grumbled.

"Why don't I order some pizza?" Ben suggested. "It looks to me like you could use a break and some food. It might improve your mood."

"A professional wallpaper hanger would improve my mood, but I suppose pizza will have to do," Richard said gloomily. "Better order two. Melanie's appetite is huge these days. And don't tell me she's eating for two. I think she's eating for a dozen future football players."

"When the baby comes and it's a delicate little girl, you're going to regret those words," Kathleen told him.

Richard merely shrugged. "So Melanie keeps telling me. I'd better get back in there before she climbs up on the ladder and tries to hang a strip of paper herself.

She does that every time my back is turned. I finally had to turn off my cell phone and stop taking calls from the office.''

"It's after seven. Why were you taking calls, anyway?" Ben asked.

"This was earlier. I took the afternoon off," Richard explained. "I thought I could get this all done during Melanie's afternoon nap. Naturally she wasn't the least bit tired today. And then I ran into a little problem with the actual papering.''

"I could order the pizza," Kathleen offered generously. "Ben could help you.''

Ben scowled at her. "You don't win, if you're the one who plants the idea in his head.''

Richard stared at them, clearly confused. "You two have some sort of bet going?''

"It doesn't matter," Ben assured him. "I'll order the pizza and be right in. I can't wait to see what you've accomplished so far.''

Richard shot him a look filled with pure venom, then hightailed it back to the nursery.

"I love what imminent fatherhood is doing to my big brother," Ben said, watching him with amusement.

"I wouldn't do too much gloating, if I were you," Kathleen advised. "If Destiny has her way, you're heading down this same path.''

She set off after Richard, leaving him to contemplate a future that not only included a wife but babies. His heart did a little stutter-step, but the effect wasn't so bad. Once again, there was none of the expected panic at the idea.

Then he remembered what it was like to lose someone and his resolve to remain unattached kicked right back into high gear.

Forget the daydream about a house filled with rambunctious little ones. It wasn't going to happen. There would be no wife filling the kitchen with the aroma of pies and cakes and bear claws. No Kathleen, he thought a bit despondently.

Dammit, for a minute there, the idea had held an astonishing appeal. No doubt that had been his hormones trying to rationalize what *they* wanted.

He picked up the phone and called for pizza, one loaded with everything, the other plain. Melanie didn't need heartburn adding to her woes. She had enough to contend with just enduring her doting husband.

En route to the nursery, he stopped in the kitchen and picked up a few cans of soda, then went upstairs to find both women sitting side by side, feet propped up and instructions tripping off their tongues. He was amazed that Richard hadn't bolted by now. He pulled up his own chair and was about to sit down when Melanie scowled at him.

"I don't think so. Maybe you can line up the stupid stripes. Richard doesn't seem to have an eye for it," she said.

"Hey," Ben protested. "I'm just here as an artistic consultant."

"Not anymore," his sister-in-law informed him. "You're on the team."

"Why?"

"Because you're male and you're a Carlton. I want all of you to pay." She grinned at him. "And I want Kathleen to win that bet."

Ben frowned at her. "If I didn't love you so much, I would not let you badger me into doing this, you know."

Melanie beamed at him. "I know. Now, please, help before we run out of paper."

Ben took a look around the room to see what was left to be done. So far Richard had only managed to successfully hang a half-dozen strips, not even enough to finish one wall. A very large pile of soggy, tangled paper was testament to earlier failed attempts.

"Are you sure you're going to have enough, as it is?" he asked skeptically.

Melanie gave him a smug smile. "I bought extra, since Richard insisted he was going to do it."

Ben noticed that Kathleen was taking in the friendly byplay with an oddly wistful expression on her face. To his surprise, she struck him as someone who was used to being left out but who desperately wanted to be part of things.

"You know," he said mildly. "I hear that Kathleen is amazingly adept at hanging wallpaper."

Kathleen's gaze immediately clashed with his. "I never said any such thing."

Ben shrugged. "Pictures, wallpaper, how different can it be?"

She gave him a look brimming with indignation. "You can't be serious."

"You saying you can't do this?" he asked.

"Of course I can," Kathleen retorted. "But I never told you that and I most certainly never compared it to hanging pictures in my gallery."

He held out a roll of paper. "Care to show us how it's done?"

She gave him a suspicious look, but she accepted the paper and stood up. Winking at Melanie, she walked over, looked at the wall measurements Richard had jotted down on a board straddling two sawhorses, spread out the paper, cut it, smoothed on paste and had it on the wall in about five minutes flat. Richard stared at her in awe.

"My God," he murmured. "What are your rates?"

Kathleen chuckled. "No charge. Actually I did the bedrooms in my house one Saturday afternoon. It was fun."

"Fun," Richard repeated incredulously. He turned to Ben. "She thinks this is fun."

Ben kissed the tip of her nose. "I knew there was a reason I brought you along tonight."

"And here I thought it was because you couldn't resist my company," she said.

He shrugged. There was little point in denying it, not even with his brother and sister-in-law paying avid attention to the entire exchange. "That, too," he said. "Tell me what you need and I'll help. Richard, you and Melanie can go and wait for the pizza."

"I thought you were buying," Richard complained.

"Hey, you're getting two free workers, one of whom actually appears to know what she's doing," Ben retorted. "You can pay for the damn pizza."

"Seems fair to me," Melanie agreed, holding out her hand so her husband could help her out of her chair. "Come on, Richard, let's give these two some privacy."

"What do they need privacy for?" Richard asked. "They're supposed to be hanging wallpaper."

Melanie tugged him toward the door "Maybe your brother will get some other ideas," she told him. "This is a bedroom, after all."

"It's the baby's room," Richard protested indignantly, even as he followed his wife out the door.

Ben glanced at Kathleen and saw that her cheeks

were pink. "Don't pay any attention to the two of them, especially Melanie. She may not be too fond of her doting husband, but she's very big on romance these days. She's as bad as Destiny."

Kathleen's gaze caught his. "Actually I was sort of hoping she was right."

Ben stared at her, not entirely sure he was comprehending. This was one of those things he definitely didn't want to get wrong. "Oh?"

"I was hoping you might have an idea or two that required privacy."

"Such as?"

"I wouldn't mind so much if you kissed me," she told him, moving closer. "Being around those two has given me a couple of wild ideas of my own."

Ben tucked his hands under her elbows and held her in place, scant inches away, close enough that he could breathe in her vaguely exotic scent. "I thought we'd agreed—"

"Don't panic. This will pass," she reassured him. "But right this second, I really want you to kiss me as if you mean it."

"But—" he began, still trying to cling to a shred of sanity.

Before he could complete the thought, she was on tiptoe, her mouth on his. That pretty much shot their agreement to hell, he concluded, as his blood roared through his veins.

The kiss might have gone on forever, might have led to all sorts of things neither one of them had planned, if the sound of the doorbell hadn't finally penetrated the sensual haze enveloping them. He had a hunch Melanie had deliberately let the pizza delivery guy keeping ringing that bell just to tip them off that it was time to quit fooling around.

Or, come to think of it, she might have been slow to answer because she and Richard were downstairs doing the exact same thing, he decided, smiling.

"Pizza's here," Richard called up, sounding faintly distracted.

Melanie gazed around, looking dazed. "We didn't get the first sheet of wallpaper hung."

"Hey, let them hire somebody," Ben said unrepentantly. "My brother's rich enough."

"I wanted to help," she said, that odd wistful note back in her voice.

He regarded her with surprise. "Why?"

When she didn't reply at once, he took a stab at it. "Because it would make you feel like you're part of the family?"

She nodded slowly. "Silly, isn't it? It's not as if they're family."

"It's not silly at all," he said, wondering again about the mother who could send her into a rage and the marriage she refused to discuss. "We'll make this our baby gift and come back and finish it."

Her eyes brightened. "Really?"

"Sure. Why not?" He winked at her. "As long as me helping you doesn't mean you've won our bet."

She laughed. "No, I'll give you a pass this time. I have a few other tricks up my sleeve, anyway."

Ben shook his head. "Why doesn't that surprise me?"

Chapter Eight

Kathleen felt an unfamiliar sort of contentment stealing through her as she sat around the kitchen table with Ben, Richard and Melanie until nearly midnight. The pizza was long gone, every single slice of it. She had a nice burst of energy thanks to the caffeine in the diet sodas she'd consumed. And Melanie was making noises about wanting to make ice-cream sundaes, though so far she hadn't summoned the energy to move. It all felt comfortable and friendly, the way a family was supposed to be.

She'd had that same feeling earlier in the nursery, which was why she'd volunteered to help with the wallpaper. She'd had an uncontrollable need to be a part of the anticipation for this new baby. She'd seen all the questions in Ben's eyes when she'd said as much, but thankfully he'd simply agreed to work with her, rather than pestering her for answers. She wasn't sure she could have explained her reasons, anyway.

"I think we should be letting you get to bed," Ben told Melanie. "You have to be exhausted."

She gave him a disgusted look. "From doing what? Richard won't let me work more than a couple of hours at my PR business in the morning. You saw how he is about letting me do anything remotely physically demanding. I took a walk around the block today, and he almost had heart failure."

"The baby's due any second," Richard reminded her. "What if you'd gone into labor?"

"I had my cell phone in my pocket and, believe me, I *want* to go into labor. This baby can't get here soon enough for me. Otherwise I might be tempted to strangle my overly protective husband."

Richard regarded her with a wounded expression. "I just want you and the baby to be safe."

Melanie's expression softened. She reached for his hand. "I know," she soothed. "Which is the only reason I let you get away with this."

Kathleen bit back a sigh that would have been far too telling. She glanced at Ben instead. "If this baby's coming any day now, we'd better finish up that nursery. The gallery's closed tomorrow. I can come by. Can you?"

He nodded. "I'll be here."

Melanie stared at them. "You guys don't need to do that."

"We want to," Kathleen assured her. "It's our baby present."

"Oh, really?" Melanie said, looking a little too smug. "It's from the two of you? Together?"

"Yes, and don't get any wild ideas about it," Ben

warned her. "It just beats the hell out of shopping for itty-bitty booties and diapers."

Melanie grinned at him. "You're not fooling me, Benjamin. You're as sentimental as the rest of us. You want to know that when that baby gazes around the room, he or she will know that Uncle Ben, the world-famous artist, decorated it."

Ben rolled his eyes at the comment, but Kathleen thought she detected something else in his expression, maybe a hint of excitement. Not until they were finally in the car and on their way to her place did she call him on it, though.

"You had a brainstorm back there, didn't you?"

He regarded her innocently. "I have no idea what you're talking about."

"Oh, can the innocent act," she retorted. "What's your idea?"

"It occurred to me that since babies like things that stimulate them and that they spend a lot of time in their cribs on their backs, maybe this baby should have a mural on the ceiling."

Kathleen stared at him in delight. "Oh, Ben, that's a wonderful idea. And when he or she is all grown up, they can tell the world that the ceiling in their nursery was painted by a famous artist."

He frowned at that. "We're not talking Michelangelo and the Sistine Chapel."

"No, we're talking about Ben Carlton and the Carlton nursery being painted with love."

"Don't make too much of this," he said, clearly embarrassed.

"Of course not," she agreed dutifully. "But is there time before the baby comes?"

"You hang the paper tomorrow and let me worry about the ceiling."

"Fair enough," she said happily. "What time should we get started?"

"I'll pick you up at eight."

"But that means you'll be driving back into town in rush hour," she protested.

He gave her a long, steady look. "You have a better idea?"

She knew what he was asking, but she wasn't quite ready to say yes. Things between them were complicated enough without throwing sex into the equation. The occasional kiss was one thing, but anything more? Too dangerous.

The temptation was there, though. It was in the heat stealing through her, the quickening of her pulse. She forced herself to ignore all that.

"Absolutely," she said at once. "You could stay with Destiny."

To her surprise, he didn't immediately scoff at the idea. In fact, his expression turned thoughtful.

"I could at that. It would give me one more shot at getting her to open up to me, since you won't spill the beans about the conversation the two of you had."

"I should have known you'd only stay there if you had an ulterior motive," she said. "It's not enough just to be there because she could use the company."

"If there's one thing we Carltons all have in common, it's that we never miss a chance to seize an opportunity when it smacks us in the face," he said.

"Sure you do," she replied. "I've offered you an incredible opportunity, one many artists would kill for, and you're ignoring that."

"That's not an opportunity, sweetheart. It's a tangled

web I don't want to get drawn into, thank you very much."

"Be careful what you say," she warned him. "One of these days I might decide to believe you, withdraw my offer, and then where will you be?"

"Left in peace on my secluded farm?" he suggested hopefully.

"That's not really what you want," she said confidently.

"Yes, it is," he said emphatically.

Kathleen studied his face intently, then shook her head. "No, you don't."

"You calling me a liar?" he asked with a hint of amusement in his voice.

"No, I'm saying you're a bit confused and misguided. It happens to people sometimes. They lose their way."

His gaze caught hers and held it. "Like you lost yours?"

She trembled under the intensity of his scrutiny. The question called for honesty, so she gave it to him. "Yes," she said softly. "Exactly like that."

"Something tells me that tonight you came close to finding it again," he said, his gaze still on her face. "You ran up against an old dream, didn't you?"

She thought of the contentment she'd felt earlier, the sense that she was finally part of a group of people she could like, maybe even love. She glanced at Ben, then amended that—people she could trust. Because, she suddenly realized, it wasn't the loving that was going to hold her back from finding happiness. It was the inability to trust.

She stole another glance in Ben's direction. Maybe, just maybe, she was about to turn a corner on that.

* * *

Destiny was still up when Ben got back to her place after dropping Kathleen off. He found her in the den with the lights low, a seemingly untouched glass of brandy beside her.

"You okay?" he asked, taking a seat on the sofa opposite her.

She blinked as if she'd been very far away and hadn't even heard him come in. "What are you doing back here?" she asked irritably. "If you came to pester me for more information, you're wasting your time."

"Actually I came looking for a place to spend the night. Kathleen and I are going to finish up the nursery for Richard and Melanie in the morning. We want to get an early start, so it made more sense to stay in town, if you don't mind."

Destiny's expression brightened, then, as if she feared that too much enthusiasm on her part might spook him, she said cautiously, "You two seem to be getting closer."

"She's a nice woman," he said just as cautiously. "Very thoughtful."

"Yes, I like that about her, too."

He gave his aunt a wry look. "She's also damned discreet, in case you were wondering. She didn't breathe a word of whatever you said to her."

"And I imagine that's driving you crazy," Destiny said grumpily. "Well, too bad."

"I'm not trying to pry. I'm really not," he told her. "It's just that if there could be a connection to what's happening at Carlton Industries, I think maybe Richard has a right to know. Not even *me*," he emphasized. "Richard."

"I'm giving that some consideration," she admitted.

"And that's all I intend to say on the subject for now. You might as well drop it."

"Suits me," he said agreeably. "So, can I stay here tonight?"

She regarded him with an impatient look. "Since when do you have to ask? This is the home you grew up in. You'll always have a place here. You know that."

"I thought you might prefer to be alone."

"If I did, it's a big house. I could go to my room. As long as you keep all those pesky questions to yourself, I'll be glad of the company." Her expression brightened. "Tell me about the nursery. I haven't been by to see it yet."

Ben described the mess he and Kathleen had found on their arrival and their plans to finish it. When he described the mural he had in mind for the ceiling, Destiny's face lit up with the kind of animation he was used to seeing in her, the kind of animation that had been sadly missing earlier.

"That's absolutely perfect, but there's so little time," she fretted, then beamed at him. "I could help."

He stared at her in surprise. "You would do that?"

"Well, of course I would. It'll be fun. What time are we going over in the morning?"

"I'm picking Kathleen up at eight. Will that work for you?"

She hesitated as if mentally going over her schedule. "I had a seven-thirty breakfast meeting with a committee chairman, but I'll call her and cancel first thing in the morning. I'll make it work," she assured him. "This is far more important."

"Richard's not going to be one bit happier about you

being up on a ladder than he was about Melanie trying it,'' Ben said.

Destiny waved off his concern. ''What your brother doesn't know won't hurt him. He'll be at work by the time we get there, and we'll be finished long before he comes home.''

''Apparently he came home in the middle of the day today,'' Ben told her.

Destiny stared at him in shock. ''Richard left the office early?''

''It's like some sort of cataclysmic event, isn't it?'' Ben said.

''Definitely,'' Destiny agreed, then grinned. ''But I can take care of that with a couple of calls first thing tomorrow, too. He won't get out of the office till we want him to.''

''Have I told you how delightfully devious you are?'' Ben asked.

''Yes, but usually it's not with that note of approval in your voice,'' she told him wryly.

''Well, I think you're wonderful. Now we both need to get some sleep.''

''You run along, darling. I'll be up shortly.''

''Destiny—'' he began worriedly.

''It's okay, really. I'm feeling much better. I just want to jot down a few ideas before I lose them.''

''Ideas for the nursery?''

''No, nosy. Ideas that are none of your business.''

Ben sighed, but gave up. He pressed a kiss to her cheek and noted that her color was much better now, her eyes livelier than when he'd first come in. Whatever was troubling her, she was getting a grasp on it. He didn't doubt for an instant that whatever she was sorting through, she would triumph in the end.

* * *

The wallpapering was going a whole lot more smoothly than the painting, Kathleen thought as she took a break for a soft drink and stood back to admire what they'd accomplished so far.

The walls were almost finished, but Ben and Destiny were having some serious artistic differences over whether there should be any sort of ogre in the fairy-tale scenes they were depicting on the ceiling.

"I want this child looking up at happy things," Destiny said again, facing Ben with her hands on her slender, jeans-clad hips and a defiant expression on her face.

"But real life is not all happy," Ben argued. "And there are ogres in fairy tales."

"That is not something a brand-new baby needs to know," Destiny argued heatedly. "Good grief, Ben, we're not painting a morality play up there."

"And you're not going to be here to get the baby back to sleep when the nightmares start thanks to your ogre," Melanie chimed in.

Destiny nodded her agreement, her gaze clashing with Ben's. "Well?"

"Okay, okay, you win. No ogre. But do all the animals have to look happy?"

"Yes," Destiny and Melanie told him in a chorus.

Kathleen grinned at him. "I think you're overruled, pal. Give it up and get another cheery character in that corner. Peter Rabbit had a lot of pals for you to choose from. And I think this one ought to be a girl. Maybe Jemima Puddleduck," she suggested. "She's cute. That ceiling is surprisingly devoid of feminine characters. What kind of message will that send if Melanie has a girl?"

"It's not some damn treatise on society," Ben groused. "Where's the damn *Peter Rabbit* book?"

Melanie chuckled and grinned at Kathleen. "He seems a bit testy."

"I'm surrounded by women," he retorted. "Strong-minded, stubborn women. What the hell do you expect?"

"A better attitude and less cussing would be nice," Destiny chided.

"Maybe another blueberry tart would help," Kathleen said. "I think there's one left."

Ben's scowl faded at once. "Really?" he said so eagerly that all three women laughed.

Kathleen shook her head. "It's a good thing I woke up early and had time to bake this morning."

He dropped a kiss on her lips as he passed by. "A very good thing," he agreed. "Otherwise, I might have to lock all of you out of here and paint footballs and baseball bats on the ceiling just to keep my male identity intact."

"If it's a boy, you can do that when he's six," Melanie offered consolingly.

"Six?" Ben scoffed. "Four at the latest. Otherwise he'll be scarred for life by all these happy characters. A boy needs guy stuff." His expression suddenly turned nostalgic and he looked at Destiny. "You painted my walls with all sorts of sports stuff when you came to live with us, didn't you? I just remembered that."

"I thought the room needed a little personality," Destiny told him. "Richard was perfectly content with that sterile room of his, and Mack already had his walls covered with posters, but your room was a blank canvas just waiting for some attention." She grinned at him, then turned to Kathleen. "Not that it lasted long. Within a year or so, he painted over it and filled it with all sorts of jungle creatures. I had to take him to the zoo in Washington at least once a week to take snapshots, so he'd have the real animals for inspiration when he painted."

"They weren't half-bad, given they were done by a kid," Ben said thoughtfully.

Kathleen wished she'd had a chance to see his early work. She couldn't help wondering if the promise had been there even back then. "I suppose they're long since painted over."

Destiny gave her a smug look. "Not exactly."

Clearly startled, Ben stared at her. "What on earth do you mean? Those paintings are long gone. I slept in that room last night and the walls are plain white."

"*Those* walls are," Destiny agreed.

Ben's gaze narrowed. "Meaning?"

"Oh, stop scowling at me like that. It's nothing dire. Rather than painting, I had a contractor come in and replace the wallboard. The original panels are stored in the basement."

"You're kidding me," Ben said. "Why would you do something like that?"

"Because I've always known you'd be famous someday, and I know how early paintings can add to a gallery's retrospective of an artist's work," she said without apology.

"Could I see them?" Kathleen pleaded.

Destiny glanced at Ben. "It's up to you."

He feigned shock. "Really?"

"Don't be an idiot," Destiny scolded. "It is your work."

Ben faced Kathleen. "I'll make you a deal. When

we take Destiny home, I'll go down and have a look. If they're not too awful, you can see them.''

Kathleen was beginning to lose track of all the bets and deals they'd made, but this one was definitely too good to pass up.

"Deal," she said eagerly. "Who gets to decide if they're awful?"

"I do," he said at once.

"I want an independent appraisal," she countered. "Destiny, will you do it?"

"Happily," Destiny said at once. "Though I can already tell you the outcome. The paintings are quite wonderful. If they hadn't been, I would have destroyed them to protect his reputation."

"Oh, yes, you're definitely independent," Ben retorted. "I don't think so. If it were up to you, I might as well just let Kathleen head over there now."

Kathleen held out her hand. "That's okay by me. Let me borrow the key."

"You can wait a couple of hours," he told her, his gaze clashing with hers, then filling with sparks of genuine amusement.

"Besides," he added lightly. "The anticipation will be good for you."

Kathleen had a hunch he was no longer talking just about the wait to see those wall panels. The sexual tension simmering between them was its own sweet torment. She had a feeling once that was unleashed, neither of their lives would ever be the same.

Ben was still shocked that Destiny had gone to such lengths to save the murals he'd done years ago in his bedroom. He considered it a crazy, sentimental act, even if she thought she was merely showing amazing foresight. He couldn't help feeling a certain amount of pride and anticipation, though. It had been years since he'd even thought of those early paintings. Getting the chance to see them again was an unexpected treat.

Still, he hesitated at the top of the steps to the basement. Kathleen was right on his heels, since they'd all conceded that Destiny was going to overrule any objections he might formulate to letting Kathleen see the wall panels.

"If you're not going to walk down those stairs, get out of my way," she told him impatiently.

"Don't rush me."

"What are you afraid of?"

"I'm not afraid," he retorted sharply.

"Then why are we still up here?"

"Because there's this nagging art expert dogging every step I take. These paintings could be awful," he said. "I'm not sure I want to expose them to your critical eye."

"You agreed," she reminded him.

"In a moment of weakness."

Kathleen tucked a hand under his elbow and dragged him back into the kitchen. She gazed at him with disconcerting intensity.

"Are you really worried that I'll criticize them? Or are you more worried about your own reaction? Believe me, I know what it's like to realize that your own art doesn't measure up."

He regarded her with surprise. "You do?"

"Why do you think I'm running a gallery rather than painting myself? Once I realized that nothing I put on canvas would ever be good enough, it was either choose another field of work entirely or choose to live on the fringes of the one I loved."

Ben wasn't sure which part of that to tackle first. "Sweetheart, you're not on the fringes. You're right in the thick of things. Your gallery has quite a reputation for discovering new artists."

Astonishment lit her eyes. "How do you know that? Did Destiny tell you?"

He laughed. "I can use the Internet. I've poked around a bit to look at the articles that have been written about your shows."

"Why?"

"Call it curiosity."

"About me? Or about whether I could be trusted to adequately represent your work?"

"About you," he admitted. "The other is a non-issue."

"It won't be forever," she retorted, then tilted her head and studied him. "So, did you discover anything about me reading those articles?"

"That you have an excellent eye for talent, that you're a savvy businesswoman and that you're very mysterious about your personal life."

She laughed. "That's because I don't have one."

Ben wondered if that was the opening he'd been waiting for. He decided to seize it. "You did, though."

She frowned at him. "Nothing worth talking about," she said tightly. "Are we going downstairs or not?"

"In a minute," he said. "As soon as you tell me why you don't like to talk about your marriage."

"I don't talk about it because it's over and it no longer matters."

The words were smooth enough, but the turmoil in her eyes was unmistakable.

"You don't want it to matter," he corrected. "But it obviously shapes the way you live your life."

"Just the way your past shapes yours?" she replied heatedly.

"I'll admit that," he said at once. "Losing my parents and then Graciela had an impact on me, no question about it. I don't want to go through that kind of pain again, so I don't let anyone get too close." He looked deep into her eyes. "Until you. You're sneaking past all my defenses, Kathleen. I'm not sure yet what the hell to do about that."

She looked shaken by that, so he pressed on. "Now's the time to speak up, if you're going to keep the door locked tight against anything more happening between us. I don't intend to be hanging out here on this limb all alone."

"I don't know," she admitted shakily. "I don't know if I can open that door again or not."

"Because your ex-husband hurt you so badly?"

"He never hurt me," she said just a little too fiercely. "Not like that."

Ben stared at her, stunned. He doubted she realized that her reaction suggested exactly the opposite of her words.

"Kathleen?" he said gently, feeling an impotent rage stirring inside him. "Did he abuse you?"

Tears filled her eyes and spilled down her cheeks. "Not the way you mean," she said eventually. "He never hit me."

"But he did abuse you?"

"With words," she said as if that were somehow less demeaning, less hurtful. "He had this nasty temper and when it got out of hand, he could be cruel."

"Is he the one who told you your art was worthless?" Ben asked.

She hesitated for so long that Ben knew he was right.

The son of a bitch had destroyed her confidence in her own talent, probably because his own ego was incapable of handling the competition. Only an artist would know how easy it would be to shatter another artist's confidence, would know precisely how a cutting criticism could destroy any enjoyment.

"He did, didn't he? He's the one who told you that you weren't any good, and you gave up painting because of that."

"No," she said miserably. "I gave it up because I was no good."

He studied her with compassion. "Maybe instead of you pestering me to see my work, I should be insisting on seeing yours."

She laughed, the sound tinged with bitterness. "No chance of that. I destroyed it all."

"Oh, sweetheart, why would you do that?"

"I told you," she said impatiently. "I recognize talent when I see it. I had none."

"But you enjoyed painting?"

"Yes."

"Then isn't that alone reason enough to do it?" he asked. "Isn't the pleasure of putting paint on canvas all that really matters?"

"You would say that, wouldn't you?"

He laughed at her. "Okay, it's a convenient response from my point of view, but it's true. Not everything has to be about making money or doing shows or garnering critical acclaim."

"Easy for you to say. You're rich. You can afford to indulge in something that might not be profitable. I can't."

"And you don't regret for one single second that you no longer paint?" he challenged. "There's not a part of you that gets a little crazy at the sight of a blank canvas and a tube of paint? Some secret part of you that looks at another artist's canvas and thinks that you could have done it better?''

''It doesn't matter,'' she said, not denying that she had regrets.

''Of course it does.''

She brushed impatiently at the tears on her cheeks. ''How on earth did we get off on this tangent?'' she demanded, standing up. ''I want to see those panels downstairs and then I need to be going.''

Ben knew that anything he said now would be a waste of breath, but his determination to give Kathleen back her love of painting grew. He would find some way to accomplish that, no matter what else happened—or didn't happen—between them.

Chapter Nine

The wall panels in the basement were remarkable. Kathleen stood staring at them, astonished by the brilliance of the colors and the extraordinary detail. As the painting in Ben's dining room had done, these drew the viewer right into the scene, an especially astonishing feat given that the artist was so young at the time he'd painted them.

Oh, sure, the work wasn't as expert as that which had come later, but the signs of promise were unmistakable. In the kind of retrospective Destiny had envisioned when she'd saved them, they would be a treasure.

"Tell me again," Kathleen said. "How old were you when you painted these?"

"Twelve, I guess," he said with an embarrassed shrug. "Maybe thirteen. I did them when it became evident that I wasn't going to be the athletic superstar that Mack was. That made all the sports equipment Destiny had painted on the walls seem somewhat misplaced. Besides I loved the zoo and all the animal shows on TV. I wanted nothing more than to go on a safari.''

"Have you ever gone?"

He nodded. "Destiny took me when I got straight A's in eighth grade."

"Was it everything you'd imagined?"

"Even better," he said at once. "But I like the tamer setting where I live now even more. One is exciting and vibrant, the colors vivid, but I like the pastel serenity of the world around me. It's more soothing to the soul. No fear of getting gobbled up by a lion where I live."

Kathleen gazed into his eyes and detected the hint of humor. "It shows in your work, you know. These are quite amazing, especially given the age you were when you painted them, but your more recent work has soul. There's an obvious connection between artist and subject."

"You know that from seeing one painting?"

She laughed at his skepticism. "I am an expert, remember?"

"How could I forget?"

He surveyed her intently, warming her. A part of her wanted desperately to respond to that heat, to the promise of the kind of intimacy she'd never really known, not even in her marriage, but fear held her back. Ben had already cut through so many of her defenses. She intended to cling ferociously to those that were left. She finally blinked and looked away from that penetrating gaze.

"I should go now," she said, unhappy with the way her voice shook when she said it.

"Seen what you came to see, so now you're ready to run?" he taunted. "Or are you running scared?"

"Doesn't matter," she insisted. "It's time to go."

For an instant she thought he might argue, but he finally nodded. "I'll take you, then."

Kathleen was silent on the brief trip home. She was grateful to Ben for not pushing. It had been an emotional day for her, not just with the probing questions about her marriage, but with the tantalizing intimacy she'd experienced decorating the nursery. She wanted to get home and sort through all of the emotions. She couldn't help wondering if that would help or hurt. Were there any that she could trust?

At her door, Ben gazed into her eyes. "It was a good day, wasn't it?"

Unable to deny it, she nodded. "A very good day."

"We'll have to do it again."

"You have more nurseries that need decorating?" she asked, deliberately flippant because the prospect held so much appeal.

He stroked her cheek, amusement twinkling in his eyes. "No, but I think we can find other things to do."

"I don't know. Maybe we should get this back on a more professional footing."

"Meaning you chase after my art and I keep saying no?"

She smiled sadly. "Something like that."

His fingers still warm against her face, he traced a line along her jaw. Her pulse jerked and raced at the tender touch. His gaze held hers.

"I think we're past that, don't you?" he asked.

"We can't be," she said emphatically.

He covered her mouth with his, ran his tongue along the seam of her lips. Her pulse scrambled, proving that she was a liar, or at the very least denying the truth. To her relief, though, there was no satisfaction in his expression when he pulled back, just acceptance, which was something she wished she could attain. It would be so much easier if she could go with the flow, if all that past history hadn't made her jumpy about all relationships, much less one with an artist who had his own demons to fight.

"Ben," she began, then fell silent, uncertain what she could say that wouldn't sound ridiculous. Denying the attraction certainly wouldn't be believable. They both knew it was there, simmering and on the way to a boil.

And if she were being totally honest, it was also inevitable that they would do something about it. The only real question was when...and maybe how much risk it would be and how much pride it would cost her.

"Never mind," he said, apparently reading her confusion. "Take your time. I'm not going anywhere. I can wait till you catch up to where I am."

"And if I don't?"

"You will," he said confidently.

"Arrogance is not an attractive trait."

"Don't all artists have to have a little arrogance just to survive?" he taunted.

"But you say you're not an artist," she reminded him, regaining her equilibrium. "And for the moment, I have no real proof to the contrary."

He laughed. "But you seem so certain, Ms. Expert."

She shrugged. "I've been known to be wrong."

"When?"

"That's not something I like to spread around." She

gave him a thoughtful look. "Perhaps if I were to see a few more paintings, I could be sure."

"Nice try," he told her, laughter dancing in his eyes. "You'll have to be a bit more persuasive than that, though. I still don't know what's in it for me."

Kathleen fell in with his lighthearted mood, because it got her out of the far more dangerous territory they'd been in only moments before. "I'll give that some thought," she promised. "Since money and fame don't seem to matter to you, I'm sure I can come up with something else."

"I can think of one thing," he said.

He made the claim in a suggestive way that threw them right back into the same dangerous fires she was so sure they'd just escaped.

"Something other than that," she said, ignoring the eager racing of her heart.

He laughed. "Too bad. If you come up with something—I doubt it could be better—keep me posted."

"You'll know the minute I do," she assured him, an idea already taking shape in her mind, something that would render him incapable of forgetting about her for a single second without putting her own flagging defenses to the test.

Already lost in her planning, she gave him a distracted kiss. "Good night, Ben."

Before he could recover from his apparent surprise, she stepped inside and shut the door in his face.

The doorbell rang almost immediately. Fighting a smile, she opened it.

"Forget anything?" he asked.

"I don't think so."

"Sure you did," he said, stepping into the house and dragging her into his arms.

He kissed her till her head spun, then walked back outside and closed the door behind him.

Kathleen stared at the door and touched a finger to her still-burning lips. There was no escaping the fact that this latest round had gone to him. She wasn't sure whether to start plotting a way to get even or to run for her life.

Ben was getting far too much enjoyment out of rattling Kathleen. He was forgetting all about protecting himself. He needed to lock himself in his studio and get back to work. It was the most effective way he knew to block out the world.

And up until a few days ago, it had been more than enough for him. He hadn't craved anyone's company, hadn't yearned for any woman's kisses. Maybe he could get that back again.

Not likely, he concluded a few hours later when Kathleen breezed in with a bag of freshly baked banana nut muffins and a large latte. She was like a little whirlwind that touched down, left a bit of collateral damage and was gone an instant later. He stared out the door of his studio after she'd gone, fighting the oddest sensation that he'd imagined the entire visit.

But the coffee and muffins were real enough. So was the edgy state of arousal in which he found himself.

"Well, hell," he muttered and tried to go back to work.

Inspiration eluded him. All he could think about was the faint scent of Kathleen that lingered in the air.

She did the same thing the next day, this time leaving him with an entire blueberry pie and a container of whipped cream. His vivid imagination came up with a lot of very provocative uses for that whipped cream that had nothing at all to do with the pie.

By the weekend he was the one who was rattled, which was exactly what she'd obviously intended. He was also vaguely bemused by the fact that not once had she lingered in his studio or attempted to sneak a peek at his paintings. She'd come and gone in a heartbeat. In fact, one day she'd paid her mysterious visit even before he got to the studio. He found raspberry tarts and another latte on the doorstep, as if to prove that she hadn't even attempted to take advantage of his absence to slip inside the unlocked studio for a look around.

Ben sat in front of his easel, munching on a tart and considered not the painting he was working on, but Kathleen and these little sneak attacks designed to get under his skin without putting her own very delectable skin at risk. He couldn't help wondering if the baked goods were meant as bribes or simply as taunting reminders of her. He suspected she intended the former, while the effect was most definitely the latter.

Since he wasn't accomplishing a blasted thing, he stalked back inside, picked up the phone and punched in a familiar number. Two could play at this game.

"Studio Supplies," Mitchell Gaylord said.

"Mitch, it's Ben Carlton."

"How are you? You can't possibly be out of supplies. I just sent a shipment out there a few weeks ago."

"This isn't for me," Ben said. "Here's what I need."

Ten minutes later he hung up and sat back, satisfied. "That ought to get her attention."

* * *

Kathleen was feeling very smug about her little forays to the country. Maybe it was ridiculous to drive all that way just to torment Ben with coffee and a few pastries, but she had a feeling it would pay off eventually. He'd feel so guilty—or get so annoyed—he'd have to let her poke around among his paintings just to get rid of her and restore his much-desired serenity.

She was in the back of her shop planning the Christmas decorations, which needed to be up by the first of the week, when the bell over the front door rang. She went out expecting to find some browser who'd come inside primarily to get out of the cold. She rarely got serious customers this early in the day.

Instead, she found a delivery man.

"You Kathleen Dugan?" he asked, looking from her to his clipboard and back again.

"Yes, but I'm not expecting anything."

"Hey, Christmas is coming. 'Tis the season of surprises." He handed her the clipboard. "Sign here and I'll be right back."

Kathleen signed the page and waited for his return, feeling an odd sense of anticipation, the kind she vaguely recalled feeling as a very small child at Christmas, before things with her mother and father had gone so terribly wrong.

When the deliveryman walked back inside, her mouth gaped. He was pushing a cart laden with what looked like an entire art store. There was an easel there, a stack of canvases, a huge wooden box that could only contain paints, a ceramic holder filled with brushes. Everything was premium quality, meant for the professional artist.

"This can't possibly be for me," she said, but she knew it was. She also knew who had sent it. This was

Ben's retaliation for her little hit-and-run visits to the farm.

The delivery man stood patiently waiting.

"What?" she asked, half-frozen by a mix of anticipation, annoyance and something she could only identify as fear.

"Do you want this in the middle of the floor or somewhere else?" he asked patiently.

In the basement, she thought, locked away where it couldn't torment her. Aloud, she said, "In the back room, I suppose. Just pile it up anywhere."

When he emerged a moment later, he had a card in his hand. "This came with it. Happy holidays, Ms. Dugan."

She accepted the card, then dropped it, her nerves jittery. She managed to get a tip for the man from the cash register, then continued to stare at the card long after he'd gone.

Just then the phone rang.

"Yes," she said, distracted.

"Is it there yet?" Ben asked bluntly.

"You!" she said, every one of her very raw emotions in her voice.

"I'll take that as a yes. Have you read the card?"

"No."

"Call me back when you have," he said, then hung up in her ear.

She stared at the phone, not sure whether she wanted to laugh or cry. Instead of doing either one, she dutifully opened the card.

"For every canvas you complete and show me, I'll show you one of mine," he'd written.

Hysterical laughter bubbled up in her throat. She

hadn't thought it possible, but Ben had managed to find the one thing on earth that could get her to back off.

When Ben still hadn't heard back from Kathleen by late afternoon, he heaved a resigned sigh, climbed into his car and faced the daunting rush-hour traffic to head to Alexandria. Apparently his gift hadn't gone over the way he'd anticipated.

Or maybe it had. He'd meant to shake her up, though, not infuriate her. Judging from her lack of response, he worried he'd done both.

He wasn't entirely sure what was driving him to head over there and find out. It could be intense curiosity, or maybe a death wish.

He found the gallery already closed by the time he arrived. The window shade in the door was drawn, but he could still see lights in the back of the shop, which suggested that Kathleen was still on the premises.

As he had once before, he banged on the door and kept right on banging until there was some sign of movement inside.

He heard the tap of her footsteps coming toward the door, saw her approaching shadow on the other side of the shade, but the door didn't immediately swing open.

"Go away," she said instead.

"Not a chance," he retorted, alarmed by the hint of tears he thought he heard in her voice. "Open up, Kathleen."

"No."

"Are you crying?"

"No," she said, despite the unmistakable sniff that gave away the blatant lie.

"Why?"

"I said I wasn't crying."

"And I don't believe you. Dammit, open this door, Kathleen."

"I don't want to see you."

"Because I sent you a few art supplies?" he asked skeptically.

"That's one reason."

"And the others? I assume there's a whole list."

"Yes," she said, then added more spiritedly, "And it's getting longer by the minute."

"I annoy you," he guessed.

"Yep."

"And I ripped the scab off an old wound."

She sighed at that. "Yes," she whispered.

"Sweetheart, please let me in. I want to see your face when I'm talking to you."

"I should let you," she muttered.

Ben laughed. "All puffy and red, is it?"

"Pretty much."

"You'll still be beautiful."

"It's too late for sweet-talk, Ben. I'm mad at you."

"I got that. I want you to tell me why."

"You said it yourself."

"But I want *you* to say it. I want you to scream and shout till you get all the insecurities that man filled your head with out of your system."

"It's not that simple," she said impatiently. "Tim said a lot of cruel, hurtful things to me while we were together, that's true. But what he said about my art wasn't one of them."

"Are you so sure?"

"Yes, dammit. Do you think I would have quit painting just because of what he said?"

"I don't know. Did you?"

"No. I quit because what I painted could never measure up to what I saw in my head," she said.

Ben could hear the misery in her voice and saw his mistake then. He'd assumed they were just alike, both being modest about their talents. He'd supposed that she was good but had been told otherwise, not that she had such a low opinion of her own work.

"Maybe—" he began, but she cut him off.

"There are no maybes," she said flatly. "Not about this."

He sighed. "I'm sorry I upset you. I thought I was helping."

"I know you did."

"Can I come in now?" he asked again, wanting to hold her, to offer some sort of comfort.

"I suppose you're not going to go away until you've patted me on the head," she said, sounding resigned.

"I was thinking of something a bit more demonstrative," he said, fighting the urge to chuckle. "A hug, maybe."

"I don't need a hug. I need you to drop this."

"Consider it dropped," he said at once. "I'll haul all that stuff right back out of here tonight and toss it in the nearest Dumpster, if it'll make you feel better."

A key rattled in the lock at last and the door swung open. She met his gaze. "It was a nice gesture, Ben, even if it was misguided."

"I'm sorry," he said, his heart twisting at the misery in her eyes. She'd been telling the truth. Her face showed evidence of a long crying jag, but he'd been right, too. She was still beautiful.

She forced a smile. "Maybe we should get out of here," she said before he could set foot inside. "Give me a second to turn off lights and I'll lock up."

Something in her voice alerted him that there was a reason she didn't want him coming in, which, of course, guaranteed that he followed her to the back.

There on an easel sat an unfinished painting...of him. He must have made a whisper of sound because she whirled around and her gaze flew to clash with his.

"I told you to wait," she said accusingly.

"I know."

"I didn't want you to see it."

"Because it was meant to be a surprise?"

"No, because it's awful."

He stared at her in shock. "Awful? How can you say such a thing? Kathleen, it's wonderful. You've got every detail just right."

"No, I don't," she insisted adamantly. "Maybe if I'd had a photo I could have gotten it right. This is awful. It looks nothing like you."

As if to prove her point, she picked up the brush with which she'd been working and started to take an angry swipe at the canvas. Ben caught her arm before she could do any damage.

"Don't you dare ruin it," he said heatedly.

"It's no good," she said again.

He held her, looking down into her tormented eyes. "I can see that you don't believe me," he told her quietly. "But let's get another opinion, one you will trust."

She searched his face as if desperately wanting to believe he wasn't lying to her, but not quite daring to hope. "Whose?"

"Destiny's," he suggested. "You trusted her to be unbiased about my work."

"Not at first," she said.

"But enough to believe her when she said those old wall panels were decent," he reminded her.

She sighed and he could feel her muscles relaxing.

"Okay," she said eventually. "But only when it's finished. Will you let me take a picture or two?"

He could understand why she wanted it to be the best it could possibly be, but he wasn't sure that waiting was wise. She could suffer another one of these attacks of inadequacy and ruin it.

"Will you promise me that you won't damage it?"

"Yes," she said, meeting his gaze evenly. "I promise."

"No matter how discouraged you get?"

"Yes," she repeated, this time with a trace of impatience.

"Okay, then. I'll bring you some snapshots of me. You have till Christmas. In fact, if you want to make Destiny extraordinarily happy, you could give it to her as a gift. I never would sit still for her to paint me."

But Kathleen was already shaking her head. "No, if it turns out that it's any good at all, I want to keep it."

"To prove that you are an artist, after all?" he asked.

"No," she said, her expression solemn. "Because it's of the man who cared enough to give me back my love of painting."

Chapter Ten

Standing in her office with paints scattered around, her own painting on an easel for the first time in years and Ben's assurances still ringing in her ears, Kathleen felt her heart fill with joy and something else she refused to identify because it felt too much like love.

She didn't want to love this man, didn't want to be swayed by tubes of oil paints and a few blank canvases, so she wouldn't be, she decided. It didn't have to matter that he'd gone to such extremes to give her back the joy of holding a brush in her hand. It didn't have to mean that on some level he understood her better than she understood herself.

In fact, in the morning when she saw her work again, she might very well decide once more to hate him for getting her hopes up.

She faced Ben and caught the surreptitious glances he was casting toward the painting.

"Admiring yourself?" she asked.

He gave her a wry look. "Hardly. I'm admiring your brush strokes. You have an interesting technique, not quite Impressionistic, but close."

She laughed at that. "I'm definitely no Renoir."

"Few artists are," he agreed. "But you're good, Kathleen. Damn good."

She drank in the compliment, even as she tried to deny its validity. "Come on, Ben. Don't go overboard. You've won. I'll finish the painting, but if you're expecting something on a par with the great masters when I'm done, you're doomed to disappointment."

"You could never disappoint me," he said with quiet certainty.

She started to offer another protest but the words died on her lips. How could she argue with such sincerity? Why would she even want to? Instead, she merely said, "Please, can't we change the subject?"

He seemed about to argue, but then he said, "Okay, I'll drop it for now. Get your coat. I'm taking you to dinner."

"Why don't I cook?" she said instead.

He regarded her with a hopeful expression. "Is your cooking anything at all like your baking?"

She laughed. "It's not half-bad. A lot depends on what's in the refrigerator. I just shopped this morning so I think I can do something decent tonight. How do you feel about grilled lamb chops, baby red bliss potatoes and steamed vegetables?"

He sighed with undisguised pleasure. "And for dessert?"

"I left you a half-dozen raspberry tarts this morning," she protested. "Isn't that enough sweets for one day?"

"No such thing," he insisted. "Besides, I only ate one. I'm saving the rest, along with the extra muffins and the remainder of the blueberry pie."

She chuckled. "Maybe you should go home for dessert."

He shook his head. "I'd rather watch you make something from scratch."

"So you can steal my secret for flaky dough?"

"No, because there is something incredibly sexy about a woman who's confident in the kitchen."

Kathleen laughed. "Good answer. I'm very confident when it comes to my chocolate mousse. How does that sound? Or would you prefer something more manly and substantial like a cake?"

"The mousse will definitely do," he said with enthusiasm. "Can I lick—" he gave her a look meant to curl her toes, then completed the thought "—the spoon?"

Kathleen's knees had turned rubbery somewhere in the middle of the sentence, but she kept herself steady with some effort. "You can lick any utensil you want to," she agreed. "And then you can wash the dishes." She gave him a warning look. "And I tend to be a very messy cook."

Ben laughed. "A small price to pay. Shall we walk to your place, or do you want to ride?"

"It's only a few blocks," she said. "Let's walk."

Though the night air was cold, the December sky was clear and signs of Christmas were everywhere. There was a tree lot on a corner and the fragrance of pine and spruce filled the air with an unmistakable holiday scent.

"Do you have your tree yet?" Ben asked as they drew closer to the small lot.

"No, I usually wait till the last second, because I have to get the store decorations done first. Sometimes the only festive touch at home is a small, artificial tree that's predecorated."

He looked aghast at that. "You can't be serious."

"Why on earth not?" she asked. "It hardly seems worth the effort just for me. I'm rarely at home during the holidays, and by Christmas Day I'm usually visiting my family."

He seemed surprised. "The mother who infuriates you?"

"And the stepfather of the moment, plus my grandparents," she told him. "I can take a day of all that, then I run back here as quickly as possible."

Ben's expression turned thoughtful and then he halted in front of the trees. "I think it's time that changed. Pick out a tree, the biggest one on the lot, the one you used to imagine when you were a little girl."

"I don't need a tree. Besides, I certainly can't fit a huge tree into my house," she protested, though she was just a little charmed by the idea of it.

"We'll make it fit," he said, clearly not intending to give up. "Come on now. Pick one. I'll put it up while you fix dinner. We can play Christmas carols and sing along."

The whole idea sounded temptingly domestic. In fact, it reminded Kathleen of all the dreams she'd once had for the perfect holiday season. Instead, most of her holidays had been spent avoiding arguments that quickly escalated into something nasty. She couldn't recall a single Christmas that bore any resemblance to those happy occasions she'd read about in storybooks.

Ben's desire to give her one more thing she'd always longed for cut through all of her practical objections and had her walking amid the fragrant trees without another hesitation.

She sniffed deeply as the vendor held up first one tree and then another for her inspection. Ben did all the practical things. He tested needles and checked the trunk to see if it was straight. Kathleen concentrated on finding a tree that filled her senses with the right scent, a tree that was perfectly shaped for hanging ornaments.

When she found it at last, she overcame all of Ben's objections about the curve in the trunk. "Who cares if it's a little crooked? We can use fishing line to make sure it doesn't topple over. This one smells like Christmas."

He regarded her with amusement. "Your heart is really set on this one because it smells right?"

"Absolutely," she said, drawing in another deep breath of the strong spruce aroma. Heavenly. If the tree didn't have a decoration or light on it, she could be satisfied with that scent alone filling her house.

"I guess this is it, then," Ben told the vendor.

The man winked at her. "Don't let him put you off, miss. It's a beauty. Would you like me to bring it around to your house when I close up?"

"No," Ben said. "We can manage."

Kathleen gave him a skeptical look but took him at his word. He hoisted the tree up as if it weighed no more than a feather and despite its awkward size, carried it along easily for the remaining two blocks to her house.

Once inside, she helped him find a spot for it in the living room. "There," she said, standing back to admire the tree leaning against the wall. "That will be perfect, don't you think so?"

When she glanced at Ben, he was looking not at the tree, but at her.

"Perfect," he agreed softly.

"Ben?" she whispered, her voice shaky. It was the second time tonight he'd looked at her like that, spoken with that barely banked heat in his voice, the undisguised longing written all over his face.

The moment went on for what seemed an eternity, filled with yearning, but eventually he shook himself as if coming out of a trance.

"No distractions," he muttered, as if to remind himself. "You tell me where your stand, decorations and lights are, and I'll get those started while you fix dinner."

It took Kathleen a moment longer to come back to earth and drag her thoughts away from the desire that had simmered between them only seconds before. "The attic," she said in a choked voice. "Everything's in the attic."

Ben's gaze clung to hers a minute longer, but then he looked away. "Just point me in the right direction. I'll find my way," he said as if he feared being alone with her an instant longer.

Kathleen sent him on his way and only then did she realize she'd been all but holding her breath. She released it in a long sigh, then headed for the kitchen...and comparative safety.

Of course, she wouldn't be entirely safe until he was out of the house, but the prospect of letting him go filled her with a surprising sense of dismay. The man was getting under her skin, knocking down defenses as emphatically and thoroughly as a wrecking ball, no question about it. If he kept making these sweet gestures, guessing her innermost thoughts and doing his utmost to give her her dreams, she would be lost.

When Ben came down from the attic, Christmas carols were playing and some incredible aromas were drifting from the kitchen. The whole atmosphere felt so cozy, so astonishingly right, that warning bells went off in his head. In response, he set down the boxes of decorations and tried to remember the holidays he had spent with Graciela.

They'd been nothing like this. Graciela hadn't been a sentimental woman. She was more than content to call a decorator who would spend a couple of days and a fair amount of Ben's money to turn the house into a showcase. What appealed to her was the subsequent entertaining, assembling the right guests, doling out gifts that were more expensive than thoughtful, and drinking. Ben couldn't remember even one holiday occasion when Graciela hadn't had a glass of wine or champagne in hand from start to finish.

He tried to recall a single instance when her eyes had sparkled with childlike excitement as Kathleen's had on that tree lot. He couldn't think of one.

Once the memory of Kathleen's delight stole into his head, he realized what it had reminded him of...holidays years ago when first his parents and then Destiny had worked to assure that there was something magical about the season. He'd lost that sense of magic, that undercurrent of anticipation somewhere along the way, but he was getting it back tonight.

By the time Kathleen announced that dinner was ready, he was feeling nostalgic, despite his overall lack of progress getting the lights untangled to put on the tree. He grinned as he recalled how many times his father and later Destiny had complained about the same thing. Richard had been the one with the patience to unravel them and get them hung properly, while the rest of them had drunk hot chocolate and eaten the cookies that Destiny had decorated with an artistic flair so perfect they could have been on the cover of a magazine.

"How's it going in here?" Kathleen asked, then burst out laughing when she saw the tangled mass of lights. "Uh-oh. I guess I should have been more careful when I took them down."

He gave her a wry look. "You think?"

"I'll help you with them after dinner," she promised. "Did you plug them in to make sure they still work at least?"

"Who could find the plugs? I've never seen such a mess."

"Hey, you asked for this job," she reminded him. "I didn't ask you to get involved."

"True enough, but if that dinner tastes even half as good as it smells, I'll forgive you for every tangled strand of lights I'm expected to deal with."

"The lamb chops might be a bit overdone," she apologized when they were seated at her dining room table. "And I'm pretty sure I didn't steam the vegetables quite long enough."

He regarded her with curiosity, wondering at the sudden lack of self-confidence. "Is this something else your ex-husband criticized? Your cooking?"

She seemed startled by the question. "Yes. But why would you think that?"

"Because neither of us has even picked up a fork, and you're already offering excuses."

She sat back in her chair and stared at him. "Oh,

my God, you're right. I do that all the time. I'd never even noticed it before." Her expression turned thoughtful. "I suppose it's something I picked up from my mother. She was always trying to forestall a fight. If she said everything was lousy first, it stole the ammunition from my father or my stepfathers. Now that I think about it, my grandmother did the same thing. There's one heck of a family tradition to pass along."

Ben heard the pain behind that sad description of what her life had been like, a succession of excuses from two women who'd apparently lived their lives in fear. Rather than being a positive role model, first Kathleen's mother and then her grandmother had apparently set her up to expect very little from men other than criticism. It was little wonder that Kathleen had chosen a man who would fit into that male-as-a-superior-being mold. The fact that she'd dumped him rather quickly was the miracle.

"I'm sorry," he told her quietly.

She shrugged, looking vaguely embarrassed at having revealed so much. "It's over."

"No, it's not," he pointed out. "You're still apologizing unnecessarily."

She forced a smile. "You haven't tasted your dinner yet. Maybe the apology was called for."

His heart ached at her attempt to make a joke of something that had shaped her life. "Even if it tastes like burnt sawdust, it wouldn't give me the right to demean you," he said fiercely. "You made the effort to make a nice meal. That's the only thing that counts."

She stared at him, her eyes filled with wonder. "You really mean that, don't you?"

Wishing there weren't a whole expanse of table between them so he could reach for her hand, he nodded. "Every word," he said gently.

Then he picked up his fork and took his first bite of the perfectly grilled, perfectly seasoned lamb and sighed with genuine pleasure. "I should be grateful for that bad example your mother set for you," he told her. "Something tells me it's the reason you learned to cook like a gourmet chef."

The delight that filled her eyes was like the sun breaking through after a storm. It filled him with a matching joy...along with the desire to strangle a few more people on her behalf. But maybe he didn't need to do that. Maybe all he needed to do was to teach her that she was worthy of being treated well. Then if he left—no, when he left—she would be ready for and open to the man who could make all her dreams come true.

Kathleen lay awake most of the night thinking about the evening she'd just spent with Ben. It might well have been the most perfect evening of her entire life.

It wasn't just about the Christmas tree that they'd managed to finish decorating after two in the morning. Nor was it about the laughter they'd shared or the gentle teasing. While all of that had been special, it had paled compared to the gift he'd given her—the reminder that she deserved to be treated well. It was something she'd always known intellectually, something she'd been smart enough to see when she'd ended her marriage, but experiencing it again and again with every word Ben uttered, with every deed he did finally made the lesson sink in.

It was funny how she'd always insisted on respect professionally, knew that she commanded it even as a rank amateur in an elite circle of very discerning gallery owners, but she'd never expected or demanded it as a woman. Ben was right. It was what she'd learned at her mother's knee and it was past time she put it behind her.

Oddly, she thought she'd done that simply by having the strength to end her marriage, but that hadn't gone far enough. The fear of repeating the same mistake had kept her from moving on, from allowing another man the chance to get close. How ironic that the one who'd breached her reserve was a man who had scars of his own from the past. She wondered if he knew how deeply they continued to affect his own choices.

Since she'd sent Ben home the night before with leftover mousse, she'd decided against taking a run out to the farm this morning. That gave her a few extra minutes to linger over coffee and the rare treat of one of the leftover banana nut muffins she'd made earlier in the week for Ben.

She was still savoring the last bite when the doorbell rang. Glancing at her watch, she was surprised to see that it was barely seven-thirty. Who on earth dropped in at that hour?

She opened the front door to find Destiny standing there, looking as if she'd just stepped from the pages of a fashion magazine. Kathleen immediately felt frumpy. She hadn't even run a brush through her hair yet this morning.

"Sorry to pop in so early, but I was sure you'd be up," Destiny said, breezing past her without waiting for an invitation.

"Barely up," Kathleen muttered. "Would you like coffee and maybe a banana nut muffin?"

Destiny beamed. "Ah, yes, I've heard about those

muffins. I'd love one. You've definitely found the way to my nephew's heart.''

Kathleen paused as she poured the coffee. ''I beg your pardon.''

''You're getting to him,'' Destiny explained patiently. ''Ben is a sucker for sweets. I told you that. You're handling him exactly right. I'm not sure it's a tactic that would have worked on any of my other nephews, though I did pack Melanie off to see Richard once with a picnic basket filled with his favorite foods and wine. That turned out well enough.''

The last was said with a note of smug satisfaction in her voice.

Kathleen set the coffee in front of Destiny, then brought in a muffin from the kitchen. The extra minute gave her time to try to figure out what she wanted to say to dispel Destiny's notion that she was waging any sort of campaign for Ben's heart or that she was willing to be drawn into Destiny's scheme.

When she was seated at the table again, she met Destiny's gaze. ''You do know that the only thing I'm after where Ben is concerned is his art, don't you?''

Destiny regarded her serenely. ''I'm sure you want to believe that.''

''Because it's the truth,'' Kathleen said, feeling a little bubble of hysteria rising in her throat thanks to the confident note in Destiny's voice.

''Darling, it was after two in the morning when Ben came in last night.''

''He stayed with you?''

''Of course he did. Did you think he would drive all the way back out to the farm at that hour?''

''I honestly never gave it a thought,'' Kathleen responded. If she had, she would have sent him packing a lot earlier just to avoid this exact misconception on his aunt's part.

"Yes, I imagine there was very little thinking going on at that hour," Destiny said happily.

Kathleen choked on her coffee. "Destiny!" she protested. "It's not like that with Ben and me."

Okay, so she was ignoring all the kissing that had gone on from time to time between them, but very little of that had occurred in the wee hours of the night before. A safe good-night peck on the cheek was the closest they'd come.

Destiny frowned. "It's not?" she asked, her disappointment plain. "The two of you aren't getting closer?"

"Of course we are. We're friends," Kathleen said, almost as unhappy with the label as Destiny obviously was.

Destiny sighed. "Friends," she echoed. "Yes, well, I suppose that's a good start. I can see, though, that I'll have to do a little more work on my end."

"No," Kathleen said fiercely. "You've done enough. Let it be, Destiny, please."

Ben's aunt looked taken aback by her vehemence. "Why are you so opposed to anything coming of this relationship with my nephew?"

Kathleen was having a hard time remembering the answer to that herself. It had started because she'd been afraid to trust another man. It had been magnified by the fact that Ben had a reputation as a moody, reclusive artist.

But the truth was that he was nothing like what she'd been led to believe, in fact quite the opposite. He was so far removed from the kind of man her ex-husband had been that the only thing the two had in common was their gender.

She faced Destiny and tried not to let her bewilderment show. It would be just what the sneaky woman needed to inspire her to get on with her campaign.

"It's not that I'm opposed to anything happening with Ben," she said candidly. "But the two of us are adults. We don't need someone running interference for us. You've done your part. Now leave it be. If anything's meant to come of this, it will happen."

"Even if I can see that you're both too stubborn to admit what's right under your noses?"

"Even then," Kathleen told her.

Destiny nodded slowly. "Okay, then, I can do that."

Her easy agreement made Kathleen instantly suspicious. "Really?"

"For now," Destiny told her cheerfully. "I suppose I should go along to my meeting. Thanks for the coffee and the muffin. Our little visit has been very enlightening."

Enlightening? Kathleen thought as she watched Destiny depart at the same brisk pace with which she'd entered. In what way had their exchange been enlightening? Destiny had said it in a way that suggested she'd read some undercurrent of which Kathleen was completely unaware.

She shivered in the morning chill and then made herself shut the door. If Ben left her feeling edgy and discombobulated, his aunt had the capacity to strike terror in her. Because it seemed that Destiny could see into the future...and saw a very different picture from the one Kathleen envisioned.

Kathleen was dreaming of a wildly successful showing of Ben Carlton paintings in her gallery, while Destiny was clearly picturing the two of them living happily ever after. Kathleen didn't even want to contemplate that image, because it was quickly becoming far too tempting to resist.

Chapter Eleven

With Destiny's visit still fresh in her mind, Kathleen made a decision that she needed to seal this deal with Ben to show his paintings. The sooner that was done, the sooner she'd be able to get him—and his clever, matchmaking aunt—right back out of her life. Of course, solitude no longer held the appeal it once had, but she'd get used to it again.

She was sitting at her desk trying very hard not to look at her half-finished portrait of Ben, when the bell on the outer door rang. Heading into the gallery, she plastered a welcoming smile on her face, a smile that faltered when she found not the expected customer but her mother.

Shocked, it took her a moment to compose herself before she finally spoke, drawing her mother's attention away from the most dramatic of Boris's paintings.

"Mother, this is a surprise. What on earth are you

doing here?'' she asked, trying to inject a welcoming note into her voice when all she really felt was dismay. She'd expected that if her mother ever did show up in Alexandria, it certainly wouldn't be without warning.

''I decided to take you up on your invitation to visit.'' Prudence tilted her head toward the large painting. ''I can't say that I like it, but it's quite impressive, isn't it?''

''The critic from the Washington paper called it a masterpiece,'' Kathleen said. She still had the uneasy sense that her mother was merely making small talk, that at any second the other shoe would drop and land squarely on Kathleen's head.

''I know,'' Prudence replied. ''I read his review.''

That was the second shock of the morning. ''You did?''

Her mother gave her an impatient look. ''Well, of course, I did. Your grandfather finds every mention of your gallery on the Internet and prints the articles out for me.''

''He does?''

Her mother's impatience turned to what seemed like genuine surprise. ''What did you think, darling, that we didn't care about you?''

''As a matter of fact, yes,'' Kathleen said. ''I thought you all thoroughly disapproved of what I was doing.''

Her mother gave her a sad look. ''Yes, I can see why it must have seemed that way, since none of us have come down here. I'm sorry, Kathleen. It was selfish of us. We wanted you back home, and we all thought this would pass, that it was nothing more than a little hobby.''

Kathleen felt the familiar stirring of her temper at

the casual dismissal of her career. "It's not," she said tightly.

"Yes, I can see that now. The gallery is as lovely as any I've ever seen, and you've made quite a success of it. You obviously inherited your grandfather's business genes."

Kathleen had never expected her mother to make such an admission. The morning was just full of surprises, she thought.

"I have to wonder, though," her mother began.

Ah, Kathleen thought, here it comes. She should have known that the high praise couldn't possibly last. She leveled a look into her mother's eyes, anticipating the blow that was about to fall.

"Yes?" she said, her tension unmistakable.

"What about your own art, Kathleen? Have you let that simply fall by the wayside?"

"My art?" she echoed weakly. Where on earth had that come from? If everyone back home had thought the gallery was little more than a hobby, they'd clearly considered her painting to be nothing more than an appropriate feminine pastime. Not one of her paintings had hung on the walls at home, except in her own room. She'd taken those with her when she'd married, but had soon relegated them to the basement when Tim had been so cruelly critical. Most had gone to the dump even before the marriage ended. She couldn't bear to look at them.

She met her mother's gaze. "Why on earth would you ask about my art? You always dismissed it, just as you have the gallery."

"I most certainly did not," her mother replied with more heat than Kathleen had heard in her voice in years. "I always thought you were quite talented."

"If you did, you certainly never said it," Kathleen pointed out. "Not once, Mother."

Her mother appeared genuinely shaken by the accusation. "I didn't?"

"Never."

"I suppose I didn't want to get your hopes up," her mother said, her expression contrite. "It's a very difficult field in which to succeed. I should know."

Shock, which had been coming in waves since her mother walked into the gallery, washed over Kathleen again. "What on earth are you saying?"

"You never saw anything I painted, did you?" her mother asked.

"No," Kathleen said, reeling from this latest bombshell. "In fact, I had no idea you'd ever held a paintbrush."

"Actually I took lessons from a rather famous artist in Providence for years," her mother said as if it were of little consequence.

"You did?" Kathleen asked weakly. "When?"

"Before you were born. In fact, once I married, I never painted again. Your father thought it was a waste of time and money." She gave Kathleen another of those looks filled with sorrow. "I'd like to think that you inherited your talent from me, though. It broke my heart when you gave it up because of that awful husband of yours. I hated seeing you make the same mistake I had."

Kathleen suddenly felt faint. Too many surprises were being thrown at her at once. "I think I need to sit down," she said. "Come on into my office."

Her mother followed her, then stopped in the doorway. Kathleen heard her soft gasp, and turned. Prudence was staring at the portrait.

"You did that, didn't you?" her mother asked, her eyes ablaze with excitement.

Kathleen nodded. "It's far from finished," she said, unable to keep a defensive note from her voice.

"But it's going to be magnificent." When Prudence turned back to Kathleen, her eyes were filled with tears. "I am so proud of you. You've done what I was never able to do. You've taken your life back, after all."

Puzzled, Kathleen stared at her mother. "I don't understand."

"I think you do. You're a survivor, Kathleen. I haven't been."

"Of course you are," Kathleen replied heatedly. "You're *here,* despite everything that happened to you. You don't have to be a victim ever again. And if painting really did mean so much to you, then do it. I'll buy you everything you need myself. I'll pass on the gift that was given to me."

Her mother gave her a quizzical look. "Oh?"

For the first time in her life, Kathleen felt this amazing sense of connection to her mother. She went to stand beside her and put an arm around her waist. "Ben bought paints for me—just yesterday, in fact. He's the one who gave me the confidence to try again. That portrait is the first thing I've painted in years."

"Tell me about this Ben," her mother said. "Is he someone very special?"

"Yes," Kathleen said simply.

Her mother gazed knowingly into her eyes. "He's the man in the portrait, isn't he?"

"Yes."

"And you love him." It wasn't a question at all, but a clear statement of fact.

"No," Kathleen said at once, then sighed. "Maybe."

Her mother tapped the canvas with a perfectly manicured nail. "The truth is right here, darling."

Kathleen studied the painting and tried to guess what her mother had seen. Even in the portrait's unfinished state, Ben appeared strong. Kindness shone in his eyes. Had it been painted with a sentimental brush? Most likely.

"I don't want to love him," Kathleen admitted at last.

"Why not?"

"Because he's an artist," she explained.

To her surprise, her mother laughed. "Not all artists are as unpredictable and awful as Tim was, you know. There are bad apples in every barrel. Goodness knows, I've found more than my share in a great many walks of life, but you can't taint a whole profession because of it."

For the first time, Kathleen understood the optimism that underscored her mother's repeated attempts to find the perfect match. "I just realized something, Mother."

"What's that?"

"You're the one who's the real survivor. You've made some fairly awful choices—"

"An understatement," her mother confirmed.

"But you haven't closed your heart," Kathleen explained. "I did."

Her mother gave her a squeeze. "Then it's time you took another chance on living. I'd like to meet this young man of yours. He has a kind face."

Kathleen smiled. "He does, doesn't he? And the best part of all is that he has a kind soul."

And maybe, just maybe she could be brave enough

to put that kindness to the test and give him a chance…if he wanted one. Now there, she thought, was the sixty-four-thousand-dollar question.

"Stay here for a few days, Mother. Meet Ben," she pleaded.

"Not this time," Prudence said. "But I will come again soon."

"Promise?"

"Absolutely. The ice is broken now. It won't be so difficult next time. Perhaps your grandparents will come, too."

"I'd like you to meet Ben's aunt, too. She's a remarkable woman, and she's an artist, as well. I think the two of you would hit it off." She imagined the two women sitting in the sunshine on the coast of France, easels in front of them. She could see the image quite vividly. It made her smile.

Her mother gave her a fierce hug. For the first time in years and years, Kathleen felt that she had a real mother again. Not that there weren't likely to be bumps in the road. They were both, after all, strong-willed people in their own very different ways. But today had given them a fresh start, and Ben, even though he hadn't been here, had played an amazing part in that. It was just one more thing she owed him for.

Ben was feeling fairly cranky, and he wasn't entirely certain why. Okay, that was a lie. He knew precisely why he'd been growing increasingly irritable over the past week. He was growling at everyone who dared to call or come by. Even the usually unflappable Mack had commented on his foul temper and taken a wild stab at the reason for it.

"Something tells me you haven't seen Kathleen

lately," Mack had observed in midconversation. "Do yourself a favor and go see her or call her. Do something. Otherwise the rest of us are going to have to start wearing protective gear when we come around."

This last was a reference to the mug Ben had tossed across his studio at Mack's untimely interruption of his work. Not that his work was going all that well, but he was sick of people turning up without so much as a phone call to warn him. Not that Mack had ever called ahead. He just brought food to pacify his beast of a younger brother.

"My mood has nothing to do with Kathleen," Ben had all but shouted.

"If you say so," Mack responded mildly.

"I say so."

Mack had wandered around the studio, careful to keep a safe distance away from Ben, then asked casually, "Have you slept with her yet?"

Ben's gaze shot to his brother. If Mack had been closer, he'd have slammed him in the jaw for asking something like that. Fortunately for both of them, there was enough distance between them that it didn't seem worth the effort. Besides, Mack still had a few quick moves left over from his football days. Ben probably wouldn't have caught him squarely on the jaw, anyway.

He scowled at Mack instead. "Do you think I'd tell you if I had?"

Mack, damn him, had grinned. "You haven't, then. I figured as much. You need to make your move, pal. I think you can chalk this black mood of yours up to suppressed hormones."

"I think I can chalk it up to an interfering brother

who doesn't know when to mind his own damn business.''

Mack had shrugged. ''That, too.'' He'd headed for the door, then. ''Think about it, bro. If the woman's tying you up in knots like this, it's time to do something about it. Stop sitting on the fence. Get her into your bed or out of your life.''

Ever since Mack had walked out, Ben had thought of very little else. It was true. He wanted to make love to Kathleen, had wanted to for a long time now. Hell, he'd even started to miss her popping up out here, pestering him, bringing along those delectable baked goods of hers.

And despite all of her declarations reminding him to keep things professional, he was all but certain she was going just about as crazy as he was.

He'd eaten every last muffin, every scone, the rest of the blueberry pie and all those raspberry tarts, all the while mentally grumbling that if she kept it up, he was going to gain twenty pounds before Christmas.

And yet, when no further pastries had appeared, he'd felt oddly bereft. The running he'd been doing to burn off calories suddenly had to burn off the restless frustration that plagued him.

Mack was right. He needed to do something and he needed to do it now.

As if Kathleen were once more attuned to his thoughts, he heard her car tearing up the driveway, taking it at a reckless speed that only she dared. He'd mentioned that more than once, his heart in his throat, but she'd remained oblivious to his entreaties. Because he hadn't wanted to get into why her driving terrified him, he let it pass each time. Today she seemed to be in a particular hurry.

Ben stood up, but hesitated rather than going outside to wait for her. When she skidded to a stop mere inches from the side of the barn, he bit back another lecture and counted to ten instead, waiting for his thumping heartbeat to slow down to normal before going to greet her.

She bounded out of the car with long-legged strides, then tossed a bag in his direction. One whiff and her driving no longer mattered. He'd reminded her of a particular fondness for blueberries over dinner the other night, and he knew exactly what he'd find in the bag…homemade blueberry muffins this time.

She handed him a cup of his favorite latte as well, acting for all the world as if it had been only yesterday when they'd last parted. He wasn't sure whether to be charmed or annoyed by that.

"I can't stay but a minute, but something amazing happened earlier this morning and I couldn't wait to come out to tell you about it."

"You could have called."

"Not about this. And since I was coming, I stopped long enough to bake the muffins so I wouldn't arrive empty-handed. I wanted to get them out here while they're still warm from the oven."

"And that's why you drove like a bat out of hell?" he asked testily.

"No, I drove that way because I enjoy it," she replied, undaunted by his disapproval.

"If you slowed down, you might enjoy the land-scape."

"I do enjoy it."

"How? It must pass in a blur."

She gave him an innocent smile. "All I have to do

is think about that painting in your dining room and it all comes back to me.''

Ben shook his head at the sneaky way she'd brought the conversation right back to the same old point. ''We've been over this more than once. Flattery, muffins and latte are not going to get you inside the studio, sweetheart.''

''What will?'' she asked curiously. ''Is there some trick I'm missing?''

''Just one. A sincere promise to forget about trying to talk me into selling what's in there.''

She shrugged. ''Sorry, no can do.''

''Since you knew that would be the outcome even before you asked that question, let's not belabor it. Why don't you tell me about this amazing thing that happened this morning.''

''My mother came to my gallery.''

He regarded her intently, looking for evidence of the simmering outrage that usually followed any contact with her mother. He saw none. In fact, her eyes were shining. ''I take it that it went well.''

''Better than that,'' she said excitedly. ''I think we're finally starting to communicate. For the first time in years, I can actually see a woman I could like, not just the mother I'm supposed to love.''

''What brought on this astonishing turnaround?''

''Believe it or not, your portrait had a lot to do with it.'' She told him about their conversation, about her discovery that her mother had once painted, too. ''And I never knew. Isn't that amazing?''

''Amazing,'' he agreed, enjoying the fire in her eyes and wishing somehow that he'd been the one to put it there.

''Well, that's all I came to tell you,'' she said.

"Since you still won't let me into the studio, I guess I'll be off now. One victory is probably the best I can hope for in a single day."

"Aren't you getting tired of driving all this way just to have me rebuff you?" he asked curiously.

"Not really," she said, then added with a wink, "Catching a glimpse of all that scenery is worth it."

Ben shook his head. "I have no idea what to make of you."

"I'm a pretty straightforward woman. When I see something I want, I go after it."

Ben noted the accompanying gleam in her eye. It made him wonder once again if what she wanted was still his art...or him. There was one way to find out, a way he'd been avoiding for some time now, because he was terrified to go down that particular path again. Each time he had before had left him rattled and uneasy. He struggled with himself once more, told himself it would be foolish to tempt fate by taking his brother's advice and plunging into a relationship that was bound to butt headlong into the brick wall around his heart.

But when he couldn't stand it one second longer, he kissed her, a hard, demanding kiss that drove his senses crazy and made his heart pound.

Big mistake. No, *huge* mistake. If she'd been in his head all morning long, now she was in his blood. He couldn't seem to get enough of her.

When he finally released her, she stared at him, clearly dazed.

"What? Why?" She shook her head, then asked more steadily. "What was that for?"

"It was a long time coming," he said, then raked his hand through his hair.

"You've kissed me before," she reminded him.

"I remember."

"But not quite like that," she admitted. "As if you wanted more."

Because he couldn't deny it, he said only, "I think you should probably go now."

"Oh, no, you don't. You don't kiss me like that and then dismiss me as if nothing important happened," she retorted.

He heard the exasperation in her voice and smiled. "Do you want to talk it to death?"

"Yes," she said stubbornly. "That's exactly what I want."

To shut her up, he kissed her again. This time when he released her, she didn't ask a single thing. Instead, she whirled around and headed for her car.

"Leaving?" he inquired.

She scowled at him. "Yes, I am."

Ben thought he was home free, until she faced him.

"Come and see my gallery tonight. I mean really look at it," she said in a tone that was less invitation than command. "You promised you would weeks ago and you've barely glanced around when you've been by there."

It was true. He hadn't wanted to look around. If he had, he might have been tempted to give her her way, to let her show his work.

"I'll fix you dinner after," she coaxed.

Ben regarded her doubtfully. "And spend the rest of the evening giving me your best sales pitch, I imagine. Or do you have more Christmas lights that need untangling?"

"Quite a few at the shop, as a matter of fact, but we'll save those for another day. I've finished the decorating for this year, anyway. No, tonight will be all about you and me." She grinned and held her fingers less than an inch apart. "And maybe just a tiny bit about your art."

Ben gazed into her eyes. If he was going to get dragged deeper and deeper into this web she was spinning around him, then he had a far more intriguing way they could spend the evening, one that was every bit as long overdue as those heated kisses they'd just shared.

With Mack's advice still ringing in his ears, he moved closer, then lifted his hand and swept a finger along her cheek. He felt the skin heat, felt her tremble. "Make love with me, instead," he suggested, gazing into her eyes. "Then we'll have something much more interesting to discuss."

Color climbed into her cheeks, but her steady gaze never wavered. Then she politely held out her hand as if they were closing some very proper business arrangement.

"Deal," she said, taking him by surprise.

Ben closed his hand around hers and felt the shock of the contact slam through him. Making love with this woman was going to be an extraordinary, life-altering experience. He should have been terrified by that knowledge, but he wasn't. The desire that had been simmering ever since he'd kissed her the very first time reached a boil.

"You're sure? You're not going to lure me into town, then change your mind?"

She regarded him indignantly. "Dugans never back out on a business contract."

"I'm not sure that business describes what we're talking about," Ben said wryly.

"It may not be directly business-related," she agreed. "But a verbal contract is binding where I come from. I don't take them lightly, no matter the context."

"Well then, I guess we have ourselves an iron-clad contract, Kathleen."

Eyes flashing, she met his gaze. "Assuming you Carltons have the same kind of integrity as the Dugans."

Ben laughed. "Oh, sweetheart, I think in this instance you can most definitely count on me living up to my word. I've been waiting a very long time to complete this particular transaction."

Chapter Twelve

Kathleen was more jittery than she had been on her first date way back in junior high school. She told herself it was the prospect of making love with Ben that had her so jumpy, but the truth was, she was almost as anxious about his opinion of the gallery. She harbored this faint hope that if he really, truly looked around he'd have confidence that she could showcase his work in a professional way that would guarantee he'd be treated seriously and respectfully by the art world.

She spent the entire afternoon polishing and dusting, adjusting the lighting on Boris's paintings, rearranging the tastefully elegant Christmas decorations she'd completed only the day before.

When the doorbell jangled just before three, she nearly jumped out of her skin, but it was Melanie who came in, not Ben. She immediately noticed Kathleen's undisguised disappointment.

"Expecting someone else?" Melanie asked, then grinned.

"Not really," Kathleen said, struggling for nonchalance. Ben wasn't due for a few more hours, actually.

"Oh? I heard my brother-in-law might be dropping by."

Filled with dismay, Kathleen stared at her. "How on earth did you hear that? We just set it up a couple of hours ago."

"Carlton grapevine," Melanie said succinctly. "Ben mentioned something to Destiny about coming into town. Then he happened to speak to Mack, who already knew and guessed that he was coming in to see you. Ben didn't deny it. Then it was just a hop, skip and a jump till the news was spread far and wide. If I could get the word out on my public relations clients half as efficiently, I'd be a Fortune 500 company by now."

"How can you even joke about it?" Kathleen asked. "Isn't it disconcerting to have the entire family know what's happening practically before you do?"

"At times," Melanie admitted. "But I've kept an occasional secret. That's been all the more enjoyable because everyone is so shocked when they finally find out. No one knew about this baby, for instance. Not until Richard and I agreed it was time to let them in on it." She shrugged. "Of course, Destiny guessed, but kept it to herself for once. She probably knows down to the second when it will be born. She seems to be intuitive when it comes to that sort of thing, or maybe God is one of those infamous inside sources of hers."

Kathleen laughed. "Speaking of that, does Richard know you're roaming around loose with the baby due any second?"

Melanie rolled her eyes. "No. I made my escape from the office while he was tied up on a conference call." She gave Kathleen a sly look. "I thought you might want some advice on what to wear tonight."

"Excuse me?"

"For the big date."

Kathleen looked down at her long skirt and colorful tunic. "I never thought about changing," she said. "Is this all wrong?"

Melanie gave her a thoughtful once-over. "Not for selling paintings, but it could use a little work when it comes to seduction."

Heat flooded Kathleen's cheeks. "I never said... Surely Ben didn't say..."

"No one had to say a word. It's pretty obvious to anyone who's watched this dance the two of you have been doing." Melanie chuckled. "Don't be embarrassed. Just be glad I talked Destiny into letting me be the one to come over here. She's very busy gloating this afternoon. I suspect it would have gotten on your nerves."

Kathleen groaned. This just got worse and worse. As if she weren't nervous enough, now she knew that Ben's entire family was waiting with bated breath to see how things progressed between them tonight.

"Now, here's the plan," Melanie announced in a take-charge way that proved why she'd been able to cope quite successfully with the strong-willed Carltons. "I will stay here and take care of business, while you run home to change. I won't let anyone steal the paintings or mess up anything. Just get back here so I can get home before Richard figures out I've disappeared. I usually go home about this time and supposedly nap for an hour. He doesn't call, because he doesn't want to wake me." She shrugged. "I let him think that, so I can get a few errands done before he gets all crazy."

"Twenty minutes," Kathleen promised. She'd grabbed her coat and was halfway out the door, when she was struck by panic. "Melanie, what on earth can I wear in here that's also suitable for seduction?"

"In your case, something that shows a little cleavage and a lot of leg," Melanie advised.

Kathleen laughed, her panic easing. "I think I've got just the dress."

"Good. Can I stick around and watch Ben try to get his tongue untangled?"

"Not a chance," she said with heartfelt emphasis. "Even if you could elude your husband for that long, which is highly doubtful, I think it's best if the Carlton grapevine doesn't get wind of the details on this one."

Ben stood on the sidewalk outside of Kathleen's gallery, unable to propel himself inside. This was it. The moment of truth. He was going in there not just to let her try to woo him into making some sort of deal for his art, but to do his own share of wooing. What the hell was he thinking? There were so many potential complications, he ought to have his head examined for even being here.

But once Mack had planted the idea in his head— okay, it had already been there, his brother had merely brought it into the open—it had been impossible to ignore. There hadn't been a chance in hell that he would stay away.

He was still staring in the window, brooding, when the door opened and Kathleen stepped outside.

"You're going to freeze if you don't get in here," she told him, amusement tugging at her lips. "Surely you can't be scared of stepping into a tiny little art gallery. It's not some house of horrors.''

He had been only moderately scared until he'd caught a glimpse of her. Then his mouth went dry and he knew the meaning of genuine terror. She was wearing a little black dress, the kind that was supposed to be suitable for any occasion. Somehow, though, on Kathleen that basic black dress took style into a whole other realm. It was barely more than a slip, actually, with tiny straps, a draped bodice that clung to her breasts, and hardly enough material to skim the tops of her knees. She had incredible knees and very long legs, slender and shapely.

Looking at her set his body on fire. He was definitely in no danger of freezing.

She, however, was shivering.

"You're the one who needs to go inside," he said, putting a firm hand in the middle of her back, then snatching it away when a current of electricity jolted through him. Touching her was not a good idea, he reminded himself. Not just yet. Not if he was expected to tour this gallery, make coherent comments, and register suitable approval.

In her strappy little black heels, Kathleen was almost as tall as he was, her gaze even with his. Her huge violet eyes were fringed with lashes that seemed darker and longer than he'd remembered. He lost himself for a minute or two in her eyes, then dragged his attention away again to firmly shut the door behind them.

Her gaze still locked with his, Kathleen stepped around him, threw the lock and drew the shade. Ben's heart started to thunder in his chest.

"Um, Kathleen, what are you up to?"

"Just locking up," she said, her expression innocent.

"So we won't be interrupted." She smiled brightly. "What would you like to see first?"

You, he thought a little wildly. All of you.

"In here," she added, as if she'd read his mind. Her eyes were dancing with amusement. "What would you like to see in the gallery?"

He tried valiantly to unscramble his thoughts and focus. "You're the tour guide," he said.

"Then we'll start with Boris's work," she said and slipped into a professional persona as she described the first painting they came to.

When Ben said nothing, she frowned at him. "You're not looking at the painting," she scolded.

He gave it a dutiful glance and concluded as he had the first time he'd seen it, that it was expert, compelling but not to his taste. "I'd rather look at you," he told her honestly.

She swallowed hard. "We're wasting our time here, aren't we?"

Ben noted that her disappointment didn't seem nearly as great as the thread of anticipation in her voice. "Sorry, but I'd have to say yes. I can't concentrate with you looking the way you do."

She regarded him curiously. "How do I look?"

"Incredible. Sexy. Alluring. Tempting."

She laughed. "You don't have to go on. I get the idea."

He searched her face. "Do you?"

The laughter died. "Oh, yes," she said huskily.

"Then we can postpone this tour?" he asked hopefully.

She nodded without the faintest flicker of regret in her eyes.

"I'll get your coat."

"I can get it," she protested.

"No, I need a minute. Otherwise we might not even make it out of here."

She sighed. "I knew there was a reason I should have put a sofa in my office."

He grinned at her. "Maybe I'll order one, something that opens up with a queen-size mattress."

"Maybe you should wait until you see how tonight goes," she said, a surprising hint of worry in her eyes.

"There's no question in my mind about how tonight is going to go," he told her. "None."

"How can you be so sure?"

Ben heard the insecurity in her voice and knew yet another moment of impotent rage at the man who'd destroyed her self-confidence in yet another area. He had a pretty good picture of her ex-husband by now, a man who took his own weaknesses and lack of success out on the woman he'd married, cruelly filling her with self-doubt, because he couldn't measure up. He'd cut her to ribbons as an artist, as a chef and, maybe worst of all, as a woman.

Ben crossed the gallery in a few strides and took her in his arms and kissed her thoroughly, determined to make up for the cruelty of another man. He could practically feel the heat shimmering through her. He pressed her hand to his chest, where he knew she'd feel his heart pounding.

"That's how," he told her gently, gazing into eyes that had turned smoky with pleasure. "It's not just the dress that's sexy, Kathleen. It's you, every inch of you. We're going to make magic tonight."

He said it with complete confidence and saw eventually that she believed him. She should. She'd definitely cast a spell over him, one that had vanquished all the heartache from his past. For the first time since Graciela's death, he was daring to think about the future.

And about love.

Even though they walked at a very brisk pace, Kathleen didn't think they were ever going to get to her house. Her whole body was virtually humming with anticipation, the sort of anticipation she'd never expected to experience again. Not even the icy December wind could chill the heat set off just by Ben's gloved hand wrapped around her own. If he'd suggested slipping into an alley along the way, she might very well have agreed without a single reservation.

Neither of them said much. It was as if words might break the spell that held them in its grip. She certainly didn't want it broken. It had been much too long since she'd believed she had the power to make a man want her with the desperation and hunger she'd seen in Ben's eyes, that she'd felt when his lips were on hers.

As edgy as she was already, it wasn't going to take much—a clever stroke, an intimate caress—to set off an explosion that would rock her. As impatient as she was for that to happen, she wanted to savor every second, wanted this delicious buildup to go on and on and on.

Despite the simmering passion, there was also a niggling doubt. Ben had guessed it earlier and tried to put it to rest, but it wouldn't go away. It was too entrenched. She didn't believe for a moment that Ben wouldn't satisfy her, but she was terrified of not satisfying him. He'd tried to reassure her that that wasn't possible, but she knew it could happen.

How many times had the heat built between herself

and Tim, only to have her husband roll away from her, cursing about her ineptitude, blaming her for all the failures in their lovemaking? Of all the things Tim had done to demean her, that had been the worst. He'd struck at the core of her, all but said she wasn't woman enough for him or for any man. And she'd believed him because she had absolutely no basis for comparison. Tim had been her first and only lover.

And her last. She'd never let another relationship get this far, had rarely been on anything more than the most casual dates. Ben had lured her out of her comfort zone, perhaps because he'd barely even tried. Tonight had slipped up on her, catching her by surprise. She'd been so intent on one goal—getting those paintings—that she'd barely even realized what was right under her nose, an attraction that wouldn't be denied.

Given all that, it was amazing that she was here at all, walking hand in hand with a man who'd come to mean so much to her, risking a failure that could rip them apart before they'd even begun.

She stumbled. Ben steadied her, then gazed into her eyes.

"You okay?" he asked, his brow creased with worry.

"Fine."

"About everything?"

She kept her gaze steady, took heart from the concern and love shining in his eyes. "About everything," she replied at last.

And she was. It was going to be okay, because this was Ben, not Tim. Tim was over. She'd been brave enough to make sure of that, even if she hadn't been strong enough to move on before now. But maybe that was the way it had been meant to be, not moving on until the timing and the man were absolutely right.

When they got to her house, she fumbled with the key until Ben took it from her shaking hand and turned it in the lock, then stepped aside to let her enter.

She was reaching for the light when he stilled her hand and solemnly shook his head.

"There's moonlight coming through the windows. I want to see you first in moonlight."

Her knees very nearly buckled at that. "Upstairs," she said unsteadily. "There's a skylight in my room." It was a gift she'd given to herself, a way to see the stars at night, the ideal light for painting in the daytime, though until very recently she'd never thought it would serve that function again.

"Perfect," Ben said.

She led the way up the carpeted stairs, then turned into her room which was, indeed, bathed in silvery moonlight. It was better than candlelight, she decided as she turned to face him.

"Now what?" she asked, her voice still shaky.

He grinned, taking the edge off her jitters. "Are you expecting me to give you five seconds to strip and meet me in the bed?" he asked.

She smiled a little less nervously. "Given the way we rushed over here, it did occur to me."

"No way, sweetheart. We're going to take this nice and slow." He grinned slowly. "You can lose the coat and gloves, though."

Kathleen shed them where she stood, letting the coat slide to the floor before kicking it aside. She tossed the gloves in the general direction of a chair. Ben's coat and gloves landed on top of them.

"Do you want a glass of wine or something?" she asked.

"You're intoxicating enough for me. What about you? Will it help you to relax?" he asked, stepping behind her to knead her tensed shoulders. "Your muscles are tighter than a drum, Kathleen."

The warmth of his touch began to ease through her, releasing the tension. "I think you're more effective than any wine could be," she said.

"Good to know."

Kathleen could almost hear the smile in his voice. "It wasn't just idle flattery, Benjamin. You really are making this easy."

"Easy?" His hands stilled. "Are you really afraid, Kathleen?"

"A little nervous," she admitted, because there seemed no point in denying it. She wanted there to be honesty between them, not the lies and evasions that she'd attempted to keep her marriage bearable.

His massage resumed, even gentler now. "Sweetheart, there's no need to be scared of anything, least of all making love. We don't have anywhere to go. There's no rush, no timetable. Nothing is going to happen until you're ready. You're with me now. There's no one else in the room. No ghosts, okay?"

His patience almost made her weep. What had she ever done to deserve a man like this? Was Ben God's reward for what she'd endured during the few brief months of her marriage? If so, she would spend the rest of her life on her knees thanking Him for His gift.

"Would you kiss me?" she pleaded, needing the fire of his mouth on hers, his tongue tangling with hers. That would chase away the last of her fears. She knew it would.

He turned her in his arms and took a long time simply gazing into her eyes before slowly covering her mouth with his own. It was a sweet, gentle kiss for about a heartbeat. Then the familiar hunger and need kicked in and Kathleen's fears fled, just as she'd predicted. Instead, all she felt was the rising urgency, the powerful pull to have Ben's hands all over her, teasing and tormenting until she was writhing beneath him.

Now she was the impatient one, fumbling with the buttons on his shirt, tugging at the buckle on his belt, reaching for taut, hot skin that felt totally masculine, totally alive beneath her fingers. The textures, the masculine scent inflamed her. She had something to prove...to him, to herself.

"I guess slow and easy is out of the question," Ben commented, laughing.

"Yes," she said, skimming her hand over his abdomen, reaching lower until she felt the hard, reassuring thrust of his arousal against her palm.

It wasn't a lack in her—had *never* been—she exulted, when she felt that solid evidence of her power to stir a man. She was enough woman for any man, for *this* man. It was a heady, exhilarating discovery. The last of the tormenting doubts from her marriage vanished. If nothing more came of this night, she could be grateful for that.

But there was more. Ben wasn't satisfied to let her do all of the exploration. His restless hands stroked and teased, first through the silky fabric of her dress, then against bare skin until her whole body was humming again, her flesh so sensitive that the slightest touch could make her soar.

When her knees went weak, he scooped her up and placed her in the center of the bed, where she was bathed in moonlight. The look of awe and wonder in his eyes was something she knew she would cherish for years to come.

"Do you have any idea what your body does to a man?" he asked. "Those beautiful breasts, those slender hips, those long, long legs? You're incredible. I don't think I'll ever get enough of you."

His words filled her heart, but it was the reverent way he touched her that made her fall in love with him yet again. That touch chased away already fading memories of the past and gave her the future.

"Come to me," she said, unafraid.

He knelt over her, his gaze warm, his smile gentle, and waited, giving her time, she knew, time to accept his body, time to yearn for him.

"Really," she said softly. "Come to me."

He kissed her then, stroked her everywhere, and when the fire was at its peak, when her blood was thrumming through her veins, he entered her with a sure, deep thrust that stole her breath.

Again he waited, patient as ever, and only when her hips moved restlessly did he begin to move inside her, leading her to the top of an incredible precipice, then waiting for her yet again.

And then, when her heart was pounding, her pulse racing and her whole body aching with the sweet torment of it, he carried her over the edge into magic, just as he'd promised he would.

Chapter Thirteen

Ben lay in bed, Kathleen cradled in his arms, sunlight now spilling over them from that amazing skylight in her bedroom ceiling. He was filled with an astonishing range of sensations that he'd never expected to experience.

Desire, of course. He hadn't stopped wanting her for a single second all night long. No matter how many times they'd made love—and he'd lost count of that— he'd wanted more. He wished he could attribute that to the long, dry spell in his love life, but that wasn't it and he knew it. It was all about Kathleen and what she did to scramble his senses.

Then there was the raging possessiveness she inspired. He wanted her to be his and his alone, even though he knew that he was incapable of making the same level of commitment. Sooner or later he was going to have to face facts—he couldn't have one without the other.

And then there was the flood of protectiveness that nearly overwhelmed him. He would die before he let anyone hurt her ever again.

And finally fear, because despite all the rest, he wasn't sure he was brave enough to risk his heart, to chance another loss. Kathleen deserved nothing less than a man who could share himself completely and without reservations, and he could lose her because he couldn't give her what she needed.

Mack had been wrong. Getting her into bed wasn't enough. Not by a long shot.

She stirred against him and that alone was enough to make him forget the fear for now. There would be time enough to worry about that when he was back out at the farm, alone, his equilibrium restored.

"Hey, sleepyhead, wake up," he murmured against her ear.

"Mmmm?"

"It's morning."

She moaned and snuggled more tightly against him. That was no way to get them both up and out of this bed, Ben concluded. Most of the ideas raging around in his head, in fact, involved this bed and a long, leisurely day spent right here. That was probably not a good idea. If he stayed now, he might never want to leave. History told him that as soon as he wanted anything that much, wanted *anyone* that much, he was doomed to lose them.

He forced himself to ease away from Kathleen and sit on the side of the bed, ignoring her little whimper of protest. It was harder to ignore the sneaky hand that reached unerringly for a part of him that had no thought processes at all, only feeling. He'd spent the whole night listening to that part of his anatomy. It was time for his brain to kick back into gear.

"Oh, no, you don't, you wicked, wicked woman," he said lightly, ignoring the temptation. "It's a work-day."

"Doesn't have to be," she mumbled sleepily.

"You'd leave the gallery closed and spend the whole day right here?" he asked skeptically. She'd always struck him as a businesswoman, first and foremost. She'd never abandon potential customers to seek her own pleasure.

She rolled over and blinked at him. "In a heartbeat, as long as you'll stay with me," she said without hesitation, proving him wrong.

Now that raised an interesting quandary, Ben decided. It left him with a dangerous choice. He opted for emotional safety, as always. "Wish I could, but I can't."

"I don't see why. After all, you keep telling me you're not a professional artist, so it can't be that you have to rush back to your studio to complete a painting."

"No, it's not that," he agreed, almost regretting that he couldn't claim that as an easy excuse, one she would readily understand. "But if I don't show my face around Destiny's this morning, she's liable to come over here pounding on the door to see for herself what we've been up to."

"Your own fault. She could only do that because you blabbed that we had a date," Kathleen reminded him. "Why you let her in on that little tidbit is beyond me."

"I didn't," he said. "I merely told her I was coming

into town. Then Mack called and asked me point-blank if I was seeing you. I made the mistake of admitting that we had a date. Foolishly, I thought he'd keep it to himself."

"And now it's costing you," she concluded, sliding from the opposite side of the bed wrapped in a sheet. She frowned at the clock. "Serves you right that there's not even time for me to bake you some muffins, if I'm expected to open the gallery right on time."

He laughed. "I think I've proved that I'm interested in more than your baking. You can stop plying me with pastry now."

She gave him an oddly sad look. "I like baking for you. You're a very appreciative recipient."

"Then by all means keep it up," he told her, not even trying to hide his enthusiasm for the prospect of more delectable goodies appearing on his doorstep. "But just for today, I'll be in charge of breakfast. I think I saw eggs in the refrigerator when I was in there looking for a snack for us in the middle of the night. I'll have something ready by the time you come downstairs."

She stared at him in shock. "You cook?"

"Adequately. I didn't survive this long by waiting around for somebody to do it for me. Don't expect much, though. Richard's the real chef in the family."

"Really?" she said, apparently finding that fascinating. "And Mack?"

"He can order takeout with the best of them," Ben said, smiling. "It's a good thing this family owns restaurants. He has every one of them on speed dial."

Kathleen chuckled. "Poor Beth."

"Oh, I think she figures she got a good deal. Mack has other attributes, to say the least. Besides, as much as Beth's at the hospital and as unpredictable as her hours can be, takeout suits their life-style and Mack's version is definitely top-of-the-line. There are no fast-food hamburgers on his menu.''

His gaze drifted to the curve of Kathleen's bare back and his body stirred again. Once more he ignored the temptation to drag that sheet off her and haul her right back into this warm, comfortable bed.

''Scoot,'' he said instead, reaching for his pants. ''You're giving me ideas, standing there looking all rumpled and sexy.''

''What ideas?'' she taunted.

Rather than tell her what she expected to hear, he said, ''I'd like to paint you looking exactly like that.''

His response surprised them both, but he realized it was true. He'd never painted people, but he wanted to paint Kathleen. He wondered what that said about how she'd managed to sneak into his heart.

Usually he stuck to nature, because of its beauty, but also because it was safe. To paint a portrait and do it well, he'd always known he'd have to get inside the person's head, to understand their soul. He'd never wanted to risk it before, not even with Graciela. Maybe on some level he'd understood even then that if he dug too deep beneath Graciela's polished surface, he wouldn't like what he found.

But with Kathleen, he already knew he'd find a gentle, caring soul. He shook off the implications of that and grinned at her. ''Now that's a painting I could see hanging in your gallery,'' he teased to lighten the mood.

''Not in my lifetime,'' she retorted and scampered quickly into the bathroom and firmly shut the door behind her as if that would end the threat.

"I remember what you looked like," he called after her. In fact, he suspected that her image was burned in his head forever.

Downstairs, he pushed that image aside and immersed himself in the comforting domestic tasks required to get breakfast on the table. Scrambled eggs, toast, jam, orange juice and coffee. Lots and lots of coffee. He was going to need it to face Destiny and what was bound to be a litany of intrusive questions. He could sneak back out to the farm without answering a one of them, but experience had taught him it was always better to do a preemptive strike.

When Kathleen finally breezed into the kitchen, she was wearing slim black pants and an exotic-looking tunic that shimmered with silver threads. It made him think of the night sky and moonlight, which of course made his pulse scramble all over again.

"What's your day like?" he asked.

"In retail you never know," she told him. "But this time of year, it's usually busy, especially around lunchtime." She gave him a sly look. "And this morning I have a tour to give."

"Oh?"

She nodded. "It's a very personal and private tour before the gallery officially opens. It was scheduled for last night, but somehow the tourist and I got sidetracked."

"You want to do that this morning?" he asked, surprised. He wasn't entirely sure why he found the prospect so daunting. Maybe it was because he was rapidly reaching a point where there was very little he could deny her.

"You're here, aren't you?" she said briskly. "And

your car is still by the gallery. I can't think of a single reason not to pick up where we left off, can you?''

There was no refuting her logic. ''You think you're clever, don't you? What makes you think it won't lead us right back here all over again?''

A slow grin spread across her face. ''I could live with that outcome. How about you?''

''It is an intriguing prospect,'' he agreed, enjoying the flash of confidence in her eyes. He'd given her that. ''But a risky one. You said yourself that it's a busy time of year. Do you want to lose business by sneaking off for some hanky-panky?''

''Oh, I think you could make it worthwhile.''

''I would do my best,'' he agreed. ''Okay then, you can show me the gallery before I head over to Destiny's, but we really do need to make it quick or she'll be joining us.''

''I'll talk fast,'' she promised. ''Try to keep up.''

Ben laughed at her obvious desire to avoid an encounter with his aunt. To be truthful, he wasn't much looking forward to it, either. Destiny was never at her most attractive when she was gloating.

An hour later Kathleen had shown Ben every nook and cranny of the gallery. He had to admit that what she'd accomplished in just a few years was quite impressive. The displays were carefully thought out, the lighting impeccable. Everything had been done with simplicity, style and elegance. The scrapbook she'd kept from past showings, the collection of glowing reviews proved that she had a discerning eye for talent.

''You've done an incredible job here,'' he told her honestly. ''You should be very proud.''

''I am,'' she said, regarding him thoughtfully. ''Is it

impressive enough to convince you to let me show your work?''

He frowned at the question, even though he'd expected it. ''It was never about your professional skill,'' he reminded her. ''It's about me. I'm not interested in showing my paintings, much less selling them.''

''Ben, that doesn't make any sense,'' she said impatiently. ''You have talent. Why not share it with the world? If you don't want to sell it, fine, but at least give other people the joy of looking at it.''

He knew it didn't make sense, not from her perspective anyway, but it did to him. His paintings were intensely personal and private, not in the subject matter, but in the way he poured his heart and soul into each and every one. He didn't want anyone, let alone strangers, getting a glimpse of the world as he saw it. He feared it would tell them too much about him. It would take something that gave him joy and open it to criticism that might rob him of the serenity that painting gave him. The world was neat and orderly on the canvases he painted, and he desperately needed to keep it that way.

That was another reason why there were never people in his paintings. People were never neat and orderly. Emotions were never tidy and predictable. And he'd been shattered too many times by life's unpredictability.

''Let me ask you something,'' he began, hoping to make her see his point. ''There was a time when you loved painting, right? When it brought something beautiful and joyful into your life?''

She nodded slowly, and he could see by the quick flash of understanding in her eyes that she already knew where he was going with this.

"And when Tim criticized, when he told you that you weren't good enough, what happened?" Before she could answer, he told her, "All the joy went out of it, correct? He robbed you of something that really mattered to you."

"Yes, but—"

"Don't tell me it's different, Kathleen, because it's not. Art meant as much to you as it does to me. So you, of all people, should understand why I don't want to risk losing that. I can't do it, not even for you. If I cared about fame, if I needed the money, maybe I'd feel differently, but I don't."

"Oh, Ben," she whispered, tears in her eyes. "It wouldn't be like that."

"Why? Can you guarantee that some critic won't rip my work to shreds? Why expose myself to that when I don't need to?"

"Then this is just because you're afraid of a little criticism?" she demanded incredulously. "That's absurd. Why would you let the opinions of people who supposedly don't even matter to you affect whether or not you continue to paint? They're not important. Tim's cruelty mattered because *he* mattered."

"You're right," he agreed. "The critics aren't important. That doesn't mean their words don't have power. I don't want to lose the joy I find right now when I sit in front of a blank canvas and envision a painting, beginning with that very first brush stroke, the first hint of a crystal-blue sky, the line of a tree. That feeling is something I can count on now. It's the only thing I can count on."

"You could count on me," she said quietly.

A part of him desperately wanted to believe that, wanted to have faith that nothing would ever take her away, but experience had taught him otherwise. People he loved went away, no matter what promises they made.

He stroked a finger down her cheek, felt the dampness of tears. "I wish I could," he said with real regret. "If ever I was going to count on another person, I'd want it to be you."

"Then do it. Take a leap of faith. Forget about the paintings. I would love to show them, and I think the show would be wildly successful, but it doesn't matter. Just believe in me. Believe in what we found last night. It was real, Ben. You can't deny that."

He smiled sadly, regretting that the subject had shifted so quickly from his work to the two of them. While one topic only exasperated him, the other terrified him.

"No, I can't deny that it was real," he agreed. "I just can't count on it lasting."

And before she could utter another word, before she could try to persuade him to stay, he turned and left the gallery.

Outside he hesitated, then dared to look back. Kathleen was standing where he'd left her, her expression shattered. He realized then that being left wasn't the only thing that could break a person's heart. Leaving was tearing his to pieces.

When Ben left the gallery, he didn't go to Destiny's. Instead, filled with anger and regret and anguish, he drove back to the farm and went straight into his studio seeking that solace he'd tried to explain to Kathleen.

Filled with an almost frenetic energy, he pulled out a canvas, daubed paints on his palette and went to work.

He began, as he often did, with a wash of blue. As the color of sky filled the canvas, his tension began to ease. He was able to convince himself that nothing had changed, that his world was still orderly. He sat back, filled with relief, and sighed deeply.

He took the time to brew himself a pot of coffee, then went back to the canvas, but this time the first stroke of the brush betrayed him. It wasn't the familiar, sweeping line of a majestic oak at all, but the curve of a woman's body. Kathleen's body. There was no mistaking it. Why would this come to him now with no photo to work from, no live Kathleen there to guide him?

He threw down his brush, tossed his palette across the room and began to pace, muttering to himself as if that alone would get her out of his head. When he was certain he was back in control, he went back to the easel.

Impatiently he tried to change the form, to add a texture that spoke of something solid and unyielding. Instead, the image softened and blurred, the very picture of welcoming arms and tender flesh.

Another tantrum, another attempt, another failure to regain control.

Defeated, he gave himself up to the inspiration, then, letting the image flow from the brushes as if they had a mind of their own. His usual palette of greens and browns and grays gave way to the inky blackness of night and the shimmering pastels of a woman in moonlight.

Her body took shape before him, as intimately familiar as the skies he usually painted. Without a picture, without her, it was her face that gave him the most trouble, especially the eyes. He cursed himself time and again for not getting them right, then sat back for a moment in dismay.

He knew in his gut why they wouldn't come to him. It was because he couldn't bear to look into those eyes and see the pain he'd put there. And that's what he would have to paint if he completed this now. It was the truth, the reality, and that's what he always insisted on when he painted, absolute clarity.

Exhausted, he finally put aside the brushes and paints and methodically cleaned up the studio, which seemed to be in more disarray than usual thanks to his impatient pacing and frequent rages of temper.

He went into the house, grabbed a sandwich, then fell into bed and spent a restless night tortured by dreams of Kathleen and his determination to throw away what they were on the brink of having.

He was back in his studio at the crack of dawn, armed with renewed determination, a strong pot of coffee and some toaster pastry that didn't hold a candle to anything Kathleen had ever baked for him. Rather than satisfying him, that paltry pastry only exacerbated his irritation.

He wasn't all that surprised when Destiny came wandering in around eight. To his shock, though, she didn't immediately pester him with questions. She merely came to stand beside him, her gaze locked on the canvas.

"She's very lovely," she said at last.

"No denying it," he said tightly, knowing she was talking about the woman, not the painting.

"Why not just admit that you love her?"

"Because I don't," he lied.

Destiny gave him a chiding, disbelieving look. "Oh, please," she admonished. "You need a real woman in your life, Ben, not a portrait, however magnificent it might turn out to be.''

"Stay out of this," he told her flatly.

"Too late. I'm in the thick of it. I brought her into your life and now you're both hurting because of it.''

"I forgive you," he said. "Eventually Kathleen will, too. Now go away.''

She smiled at that. "Forgiveness doesn't come that easily to you," she chided. "Besides, there's nothing to forgive, is there? Kathleen is the perfect woman for you.''

"It doesn't matter.''

"It's the only thing that matters," she said fiercely.

He gave Destiny a hard look. "I thought you dragged her out here because of my art. Wasn't she merely supposed to convince me that I had talent?''

"I think we both know better than that.''

"Well, whatever your intentions, it was a mistake.''

"You keep telling yourself that. Maybe you'll wind up believing it. Of course, you'll also be old and alone and bitter.''

"Not so alone," he muttered, not liking the picture she painted. "I'll have you.''

"Not forever, darling," she reminded him matter-of-factly. "And your brothers have their own lives now, their own families. You'll always be a part of those lives, of course, but you need to be—you deserve to be—the center of someone's universe. Even more important, you need to make someone the center of yours.''

"Why?" he asked, not even beginning to understand. Loneliness had become a way of life long ago. Even when his whole family had been around, he'd felt alone.

"Because, in the end, love is the only thing any of us has that truly matters."

"You've been courted. You've been admired by many a man, but you've chosen to live without the love of a man all these years," he reminded her.

"And that was probably a costly mistake, not just for me, but for all of you," she admitted. She gave him a surprisingly defiant look. "Moreover, it's one I intend to correct before too long."

Ben seized on the implication. "What on earth does that mean?" he demanded, not entirely sure he liked the sound of it and not just because he hated having his own world turned upside down, which any change in Destiny's life was bound to do.

"Nothing for you to fret about," she reassured him. "I won't do anything until I know you're settled and happy."

He scowled at her. "Isn't that blackmail? If I decide to maintain the status quo, you're stuck here, so therefore I have some obligation to what? Get married?"

She beamed at him. "That would do nicely. Let me know when you and Kathleen have set a date."

"Hold it," he protested when she started toward the door. "No date. No wedding. I am not letting you blackmail me into making a decision I'm not ready to make, will probably never be ready to make."

"Oh, for goodness' sakes, Benjamin, now you're just being stubborn," she declared, facing him with an exasperated expression. "It's the worst of the Carlton traits. Everyone has always said you were the most like me, but I see absolutely no evidence of that right now. Whatever the choices I made, at heart I'm a romantic. I believe in happily ever after. I certainly thought I taught you more about grabbing on to life with both hands.''

''You tried,'' he admitted grudgingly.

''Then why are you here when there's a woman in Alexandria who's brokenhearted because she thinks she pushed you too hard? She's terrified you'll think she only slept with you to get her hands on your paintings.''

The thought had never crossed his mind, at least not until this moment. Now he had to wonder. As soon as he did, he dismissed the idea. There wasn't a shred of duplicity in Kathleen. He wished he could say the same about his sneaky aunt.

''Nice try,'' he congratulated her. ''For a minute there you had me going.''

''I have no idea what you're talking about. I was with Kathleen yesterday after you'd gone. She's beside herself. If you don't believe me, call Melanie or Beth. We were all there.''

The thought of that made his skin crawl. ''What the hell was going on, some sort of Carlton hen party?'' He shuddered. ''Just thinking about all four of you gathered around discussing me and Kathleen is enough to twist my stomach into knots.''

''It should,'' Destiny said without a trace of sympathy. ''You're not very popular with the females of the family right now.''

''What did I do?'' he asked, bewildered. ''I was honest with her. I've been honest with Kathleen from the beginning. She knew what she was getting into when we were together the other night.''

''Did she really? You slept with her and then you walked out on her,'' Destiny accused. ''Do you think she was expecting that?''

"In a very condensed version, that much is true," he acknowledged. "But a lot went on in between." He raked a hand through his hair as he realized that he wasn't going to win, no matter how he tried to explain away that scene in the gallery. "What do you want from me? What does Kathleen want from me? Besides my paintings, of course."

"Oh, forget the stupid paintings," Destiny said. "I want you to tell that woman you love her before it's too late."

He stared at her bleakly, filled with dismay that this woman who understood him so well could ask the impossible of him.

When he said nothing, she walked over to his painting. "Look at this," she commanded. When she was apparently satisfied that his gaze was on the canvas, she asked, "What do you see?"

"Kathleen," he said. "And I've never painted a portrait before. Is that your point?"

"No, darling," she said more gently. "I want you to open your eyes and really look at what's on this canvas. It's not just a very nice likeness of Kathleen."

He tore his gaze from the painting and stared at her, not comprehending.

"It's a portrait of love in all its radiance," she told him quietly. "Any man who could paint this is capable of great passion."

After she'd gone, Ben sat and stared at the painting. He could see the passion she was talking about. In fact, passion was something he certainly understood, but love? Only four little letters, but they added up to something that scared the living daylights out of him. He didn't think there were enough weeks in a lifetime or enough reassurances to help him move past that terror.

Chapter Fourteen

Kathleen still couldn't get over the way the Carlton women had rallied around her two days ago. Within moments of Destiny's arrival at the gallery and her discovery that Ben had walked out on Kathleen that morning, she sent out an alert to the others. Minutes later Melanie and Beth had burst into the gallery like the calvary arriving. Melanie had brought a huge bag of junk food, and Beth had brought nonalcoholic drinks for Melanie and champagne for the rest of them. These women clearly knew how to prepare for a crisis.

Satisfied with the reinforcements, Destiny had locked the gallery door and they'd all proceeded to get thoroughly intoxicated on potato chips, cheesecake, ice cream and old-fashioned gossip.

Ben had not fared well, despite Kathleen's half-hearted attempts to defend him or at the very least to make them see his point of view. She'd been amazed to find them all on her side.

"Take him out and shoot him," Melanie had suggested with real enthusiasm. "Maybe that would get his attention."

"Aren't you being just the teensiest bit bloodthirsty?" Kathleen had asked weakly. "That can't possibly be good for the baby."

"Boy or girl, this baby needs to know that there's right and wrong in the world when it comes to the way men treat women," Melanie insisted. "Besides, this baby is now officially overdue and getting on my nerves. I want the man responsible for this pregnancy—no, I want *all* men, especially Carlton men— to pay."

"Don't get too carried away and do anything you'll regret. You'll stop blaming Richard once you hold the baby," Beth assured her. She turned to Kathleen and added, "As for Ben, shooting's too good for him. Tie him up and torture him. You have no idea how often I was tempted to do that to Mack, when he was being pigheaded."

"But you didn't," Kathleen reminded her, then hesitated. "Did you?"

"No," Beth said with apparent regret.

"That's because the person you really wanted to torture was Destiny," Melanie said, then gave their aunt-in-law an apologetic look. "No offense."

Destiny laughed. "None taken. But since we're obviously not going to convince Kathleen to shoot or torture Ben, perhaps we should try to focus on some more practical solutions to this dilemma. How can we get through to him? Goodness knows, I've tried. If it hadn't been for Graciela, I doubt he'd be making this so difficult, but her death destroyed whatever progress he'd made in terms of having faith that people he cared about would stick around. He seems to have forgotten all about what brought on their fight that awful night.''

Kathleen took all of this in. She'd known that the woman Ben had loved had died, but she hadn't realized there had been any sort of fight.

''Why were they fighting?'' she asked.

The three women exchanged a look.

''He never told you?'' Destiny asked.

''Not really. I just knew that he felt horribly guilty,'' she said.

''Oh, please,'' Destiny said. ''Of course it was tragic, but Ben has absolutely nothing to feel guilty about. Not only was she far too drunk to get behind the wheel that night, but they fought in the first place because he'd caught her cheating on him. It wasn't the first time, either, just the first time he'd seen it with his own eyes.''

''Oh, my,'' Kathleen whispered. It was even worse than she'd thought. Ben had suffered not only a loss, but a betrayal. It was little wonder he didn't trust anyone.

They'd all fallen silent then, Beth munching thoughtfully on chips while Melanie ate the last of the chocolate fudge ice cream from the half-gallon container. Kathleen picked disconsolately at her third slice of cheesecake. She was pretty sure if she finished it, she'd throw up, but she couldn't seem to stop eating.

''I don't think there's anything any of us can do,'' Kathleen ventured after a while. ''Ben has to figure out for himself that I would never betray him. He has to want this relationship enough to get past his fear of loss. He has to see that either way he's going to lose and at least if we've tried, he'll have had something good for a while."

"Good?" Beth asked in a mildly scolding tone. "*Extraordinary*. He'll have had something extraordinary. Don't lose sight of that, Kathleen. This isn't just some happy little diversion. It's the real deal."

It was still hard for Kathleen to see herself in that kind of glowing light. She'd felt that way in Ben's arms. She'd had a hint of it when he'd praised her painting, when he'd gone into raptures over her cooking. But those feelings of self-worth were new and fragile. It would be far too easy to retreat into the more familiar self-doubt.

"Thank you for reminding me of that," she told Beth. "You have no idea how hard it is for me to remember that, especially this morning, but it's coming back to me. I owe Ben and all of you for that."

Beth gave her a curious look. "Is there a story there?"

"Yes," she admitted. "But it's not worth repeating ever again. I am finally going to put it where it belongs, in the past."

"Good for you!" Melanie cheered.

"Does Ben know?" Destiny asked, a frown knitting her brow.

"Yes."

"And he still walked out of here and left you feeling abandoned?" she said indignantly. "What is wrong with that man? Obviously I need to have another talk with him. In fact, right now I'd like to shake my nephew till something stirs in that thick head of his."

"Don't," Kathleen pleaded, but her request fell on deaf ears. She'd seen the determined glint in Destiny's eyes and known Ben was in for a blistering lecture.

She tried to work up a little sympathy for him, but in the end she'd concluded he was only getting what he deserved. She had a few choice words she'd like to say to him herself. Too bad they hadn't come to her before he'd slunk out of the gallery.

Now, though, with the hours crawling by and no word from Destiny or Ben, she had to wonder if Destiny had failed to get through to him, if it wasn't over, after all, simply because Ben had decreed that it was. They said you couldn't make a person fall in love with you, but she didn't believe that was Ben's problem. He *had* fallen in love with her. He was even willing to admit it. He just wasn't willing to act on it, not in the happily-ever-after way she'd begun to long for. And in the end what difference did the admission make, if it wasn't going to go anywhere?

She sighed and tried to concentrate on tallying up the day's sales, but the numbers kept blurring through her tears. She needed to get out of the gallery. She needed to walk or maybe run.

She needed a drive in the country.

She sighed again. That was the last thing she dared to do. Going to Ben's—going anywhere near Ben's—was beyond self-destructive. It was stupid, foolish, pitiful. The list of adjectives went on and on.

None of them seemed to prevent her from getting into her car and driving out to Middleburg, but when she reached the entrance to the farm, her pride finally kicked in. She drove on past, then turned around, muttering another litany of derogatory adjectives about herself as she drove. She hadn't done anything this adolescent and absurd since high school.

Thoroughly irritated with her cowardice and immaturity, she made herself turn in the gate and drive up to the house, determined to see Ben and clear the air. But when she got there, the studio and house were both dark as pitch, and Ben's car was nowhere in sight.

Obviously, he wasn't sitting around alone, moping about their relationship. Why should she? She should go back to town, open the gallery and take advantage of the last-minute Christmas shoppers roaming the streets.

In the end, though, she simply went home, too emotionally exhausted to cope with anything more than a hot bath and warm milk and her own lonely bed. With any luck Ben, who'd managed to torment her all day long, would stay the hell out of her dreams.

After forcing himself to go into Middleburg to grab a beer and some dinner after Destiny's visit, Ben spent another tortured night dreaming of Kathleen and an endless stream of paintings that began as landscapes and turned into portraits, always of the same woman. By morning he was irritable and in no mood for the 7:00 a.m. phone call from his brother.

"You'd better read the paper," Mack announced without preamble.

"Why?"

"Destiny and Pete Forsythe have struck again."

"What the hell are you talking about?" he mumbled, still half-asleep, but coming awake fast.

"Get your paper, then call me back if you need to rant for a while. I've been through this, so you'll get plenty of sympathy from me. Richard, too. This is vintage Destiny. It's our aunt at her sneakiest."

Ben dragged on a pair of faded jeans and raced downstairs, cursing a blue streak the whole way. He had a pretty good idea what to expect when he turned to Forsythe's column. After all, the gossip columnist was Destiny's messenger of choice when all her other tactics had failed. Letting the entire Metropolitan Washington region in on whichever Carlton romance wasn't moving along to suit her was supposed to motivate all the parties. It was the kind of convoluted logic he'd never understood, but he couldn't deny it had probably pushed things along for Richard and Mack, despite the havoc the column had wreaked at the time.

He opened the paper with some trepidation. There it was, summed up right in the headline: Art Dealer Courts Reclusive Carlton Heir.

"But is Alexandria art expert Kathleen Dugan, known for finding undiscovered talent, looking for something other than paintings to hang on the walls of her prestigious gallery?" Forsythe asked. "Word has it that she's after something bigger this time. Marriage, perhaps?"

Ben groaned.

"That's what insiders are telling us," Forsythe continued, "but artist Ben Carlton, who rarely leaves his Middleburg farm, may be a reluctant participant in any wedding plans. Then, again, when it comes to the wealthy Carlton men, love does have a way of sneaking up on them when they least expect it. Stay tuned here for the latest word on when this last remaining Carlton bachelor bites the marital dust."

Ben uttered a curse and threw the paper aside. "It's not going to work, Destiny. Not this time. You've overplayed your hand."

He picked up the phone, not to call Mack, but Destiny, then slowly hung up again before the call could go through. What was the point? This was what she did. She meddled. She did it because she loved them.

Misguided as she might be, he could hardly rip her to shreds for acting on her convictions.

Unfortunately, he was at a loss when it came to figuring out a way to counteract that piece of trash that Forsythe had written based on his latest hot tip from Destiny. Truthfully, it didn't matter to him all that much. He didn't see enough people on a daily basis to worry about embarrassment or awkward explanations.

Kathleen, however, was right smack in the public eye all the time. He could just imagine the curiosity seekers this would send flooding into her gallery. Maybe she'd be grateful for the influx of business, but he doubted it.

He should call her, apologize for his aunt dragging her into the middle of this public spectacle, but he couldn't see the point to that, either. The one thing Kathleen really wanted to hear from him he couldn't say.

Of course, there was one thing he could do that would at least give people pause, if not make that article seem like a total lie. But did he have the courage to do it?

He spent the entire morning waging war with himself, but by noon he'd made a decision. He began crating up all the pictures in his studio. It took until midnight to get them boxed to his satisfaction. He'd gone about the task blindly, refusing to pause and look at his work for fear he'd change his mind. He owed this to Kathleen, this and more. Maybe if he gave her the showing she'd been working so hard to get, it would prove to the world that whatever was between them was all about his art.

Besides, with Christmas only two days away, it was

the only gift he could come up with that he knew she truly wanted…and that he was capable of giving.

Christmas Eve day dawned bright and clear, but Kathleen thought she smelled a hint of snow in the air. The prospect of a white Christmas normally would have made her heart sing, but today all she could think about was what a nuisance it would be when it came time to drive to Providence, where her mother and grandparents were expecting her in time for midnight services at the church that the Dugans had attended for generations.

There still hadn't been another peep from Ben. She'd thought for sure he would call when that ridiculous item had appeared in the morning paper the day before. He had to be as outraged as she was to see their private relationship played out for the entire world to speculate about over their morning coffee. Maybe he'd been too humiliated or, given the way he hid out at that farm of his and kept the world at arm's distance, perhaps he hadn't even seen it.

Despite her indignation when she'd first seen Pete Forsythe's column, Kathleen had clipped it from the paper. Maybe it would serve as a reminder that she was still capable of misreading people. She took it out of her desk drawer now and read it yet again, shaking her head anew at the idea that anyone might actually care what was going on in her love life.

For all of its juicy, speculative tone, the column had gotten one thing right. She had started out wanting to represent Ben's art and now she simply wanted him. Fortunately, neither Pete Forsythe nor his inside source—Destiny, she imagined—had any idea just how badly she wanted Ben. No, she corrected, Destiny did know, which made what she'd done unforgivable.

The truth was that Kathleen craved Ben's touch, yearned for the times when he studied her with his penetrating, artist's eye as if he were imagining her naked, in his studio…in his bed.

Despite their superficial differences—his privileged background, her childhood struggles and disastrous marriage, his need for privacy, hers for a constant, if somewhat impersonal, social whirl—Kathleen had the feeling that at their core they were very much alike. They were both searching for something that had been missing from their lives. She recognized that about herself, recognized that she'd found it in Ben. He hadn't yet had that epiphany. It was possible, she was forced to admit, that he never would.

She'd discovered in that one glorious night they'd shared that he was a generous, attentive lover, a kind and gentle man, but he withheld a part of himself. She knew why that was. It couldn't be any more plain, in fact. The strong, self-assured man she knew was, at heart, a kid terrified of losing someone important again, a kid who'd grown into a man who'd lost the woman he loved, as well. Three devastating, impossible-to-forget losses. Add in Graciela's betrayal and it is was plain why he found it easier to keep her at a distance than to risk being shattered if she left or tragedy struck.

To a degree he even kept the family he adored at arm's length, always preparing himself to cope in case something terrible happened and they disappeared from his life.

Unfortunately, Kathleen had absolutely no idea how to prove that she was in his life to stay, that her initial desire to represent his art had evolved into a passion for him, a passion that wasn't going to die. It would take time and persistence to make him believe that. She had persistence to spare, but time was the one thing he obviously didn't intend to give her, to give them. And how much good would it really do, anyway? His family had had a lifetime to convince him and it hadn't been enough. Not to heal the pain caused by those who had gone.

Fortunately, on this last shopping day before Christmas, there wasn't a single moment to dwell on any of this. From the moment she opened the shop's door, she was deluged with customers, many of them no doubt drawn in by curiosity because of that stupid gossip column. Still, she was grateful, because it kept her busy, kept her from having to think.

By midafternoon she'd written up dozens of very nice sales and cleaned out a wealth of inventory. She was about to eat the chicken salad sandwich she'd brought from home when a delivery truck pulled up in front of the gallery, double parking on the busy street.

"What on earth?" she murmured when she recognized the same driver who'd brought her the art supplies. Could this possibly be another gift from Ben? Maybe a peace offering? How typical that he was having someone else deliver it, someone else face her.

She opened the door as the driver loaded his cart with what looked to be packing crates, the kind used for paintings. As the stack grew, her heart began to pound with an unmistakable mix of anticipation and dread.

"Merry Christmas, ma'am," the driver said cheerfully as he guided the precariously balanced stack into the gallery's warmth. "It's a cold one out there. I'm thinking we'll have snow on the ground by morning."

"Seems that way to me, too," Kathleen said, eyeing the bounty warily. "Is this from Mr. Carlton?"

"Yes, ma'am. Picked it up from him first thing this morning. He was real anxious for you to get it, but traffic's a bear out there, so it took me a while to get over here." He eyed the stack with a frown. "You need me to help you open these?"

"No, thanks. I'm used to opening crates like this," she said, offering him a large tip. "Merry Christmas."

Once he had gone, she stood and stared at the overwhelming number of paintings Ben had sent. The temptation to rip into them and get her first glimpse of the art he'd been denying her was overwhelming, but she resisted.

So, she thought, running her fingers over one of the crates, this was it. He'd thrown down the gauntlet. She was filled with a sudden, gut-deep fear that this was either a test or, far worse, a farewell gift. Whichever he'd meant it to be, she knew she couldn't accept. If she did, it would destroy all hope. It would be the end of the most important thing that had ever happened to her, perhaps to either of them.

She looked at her copy of the receipt the driver had given her and immediately called the delivery service. "Do you have the ability to get in touch with one of your drivers?" she asked.

"Yes, ma'am, but most of them are coming in for the day. It's Christmas Eve and they're getting off early."

She explained who she was. "Your driver just left here not five minutes ago. I need him to come back. I know it's an inconvenience, but please tell him I'll make it worth his while. It's very important."

Apparently the dispatcher caught the urgency in her

voice, because he said, "Sit tight, ma'am. I'll do what I can."

Ten minutes later the truck pulled up outside and the driver came in.

"Is there something wrong, Ms. Dugan? Was there a problem with the shipment?"

"Yes, you could say that," she said. "I need you to take all of this back to Mr. Carlton, please."

"Now?" he asked incredulously, then took a good, long look at her face and nodded slowly. "No problem. I'll be happy to do it."

She dragged out her checkbook. "Name your price."

He shook his head. "It's on me, ma'am. Headquarters is out that way, anyway." He grinned at her. "Besides, I read that stuff that was in the paper about the two of you. I figured this might have something to do with that. I want to see the look on Mr. Carlton's face when all of this lands right back on his doorstep."

Filled with a sudden burst of expectancy, Kathleen found herself returning his smile. "Yes. I'm rather anxious to see that myself. In fact, I'll be right behind you."

Ben Carlton was not going to toss potentially thousands of dollars in paintings at her and convince her she'd won. Until they were together—truly, happily-ever-after together—neither one of them would have won a blasted thing.

Chapter Fifteen

Mack and Richard converged on the farm twenty minutes after Ben had sent the shipment of paintings off to Kathleen.

"Why didn't you ever call me back yesterday?" Mack demanded.

"We'd have been here sooner, but I didn't want to leave Melanie alone at the house," Richard said. "Beth's there now, watching her like a hawk, I hope. Melanie keeps trying to slip out to finish her Christmas shopping. I swear that baby is going to be born in an aisle at some boutique."

Ben chuckled. "Bro, I think you're fighting a losing battle. If Melanie wants to shop, you should know by now that you're not going to stop her."

Richard raked a hand through his hair, then stopped himself. "Yeah, I'm beginning to get that," he admitted with evident frustration. "I swear to God, though, I'm going to be bald by the time this kid gets here."

"It's not going to be much longer," Mack soothed. "Beth predicts a Christmas baby."

Richard's eyes immediately filled with panic. "Christmas is tomorrow. That means Melanie could be going into labor right now. First babies always take a long time, right?"

Mack looked at Ben and rolled his eyes. "Do you have your cell phone?"

"Of course," Richard snapped impatiently.

"It's on?"

"Yes."

"Then stop worrying," Mack advised. "We're here to solve Ben's problems, not to watch you panic over contractions that haven't even started."

"Just wait," Richard said grimly. "One of these days the two of you are going to be in my place, and I'm not giving you one single shred of sympathy."

"I will never be in your place," Ben said wearily, then almost immediately regretted it because both of his brothers turned their full attention on him. He should have been grateful for the temporary distraction from their obvious mission and kept his mouth shut.

"Do you want to be where I am?" Richard asked. "Remember, I was where you are for a very long time, but I've got to tell you that nothing compares to where I am now." He shrugged. "Okay, maybe not right this minute, but generally speaking being married to Melanie is the smartest thing I've ever done."

"Same here," Mack said. "Beth is incredible. Destiny's got her faults, but when it comes to picking the right women for us, she nailed it for Richard and for me. Do you really think she made a mistake in your case?''

Ben thought about it, really thought about it, for the first time. Truthfully, he knew that Destiny hadn't made a mistake. And if he were being totally honest, he realized that the prospect of having a family wasn't half as scary as it had once been.

"No, there's no mistake," he admitted.

"Then what are you going to do about it?" Mack asked. "You're not going to accomplish what you want sitting around out here. The woman I presume you want to have a family with is probably packing her bags for Providence right about now."

"Providence?" Ben echoed. "Why?"

"Destiny says Kathleen is going to spend the holidays with her family," Richard told him. "She's worried she might decide not to come back."

Ben couldn't imagine such a thing. Kathleen would never close the gallery she loved and move back home. "That's just Destiny trying to get me all worked up," he said confidently.

"You willing to take a chance that she's wrong?" Richard asked, just as his cell phone rang. He jumped as if he'd been shocked, fumbled to get it out of his pocket, then dropped it.

"Good grief, man, she'll have the baby before you get yourself together," Mack told him with a shake of his head. He picked up the phone and handed it to Richard.

"Yes? Are you okay?" Richard demanded when he finally answered the phone.

The color immediately washed out of his face. "I'm on my way," he said, turning the phone off and jamming it back into his pocket. "The baby…" He dragged his hand through his hair again. "My God, the baby's coming. I have to get home. We have a plan. How are we going to follow the plan if I'm not even there?"

"Beth is there," Mack reminded him. "She's a doctor."

"But the plan," Richard protested. "It was all written out so we wouldn't forget anything."

"Melanie knows this plan, right?"

"Sure, but—"

Ben stared at the sight of his cool, unflappable brother basically falling apart in front of him. Mack immediately took charge.

"Forget the damn plan," Mack said. "Let's just go." He steered Richard toward the car.

"I'll follow you," Ben said.

Mack nodded toward the driveway and the plume of dust that was being kicked up. "You might want to reconsider that, pal. Looks to me like company's coming."

"Company?" Ben echoed blankly, then saw a familiar delivery truck and right on its tail an even more familiar car being driven by a sexy, speed-crazed maniac. His heart leaped into his throat, but this time the reaction had less to do with fear than it did with pure, unadulterated delight.

Maybe he hadn't ended this thing with Kathleen, after all. And given the mushy way he was feeling about babies and family right now, it was a damn good thing.

Even as Mack tore away from the house, Ben watched with bated breath as the delivery truck pulled up next to the studio. Kathleen's sporty little car screeched to a halt right beside it. She bounded out of the car with eyes blazing and headed straight for him.

"What is *that* all about?" she demanded, gesturing toward the van. The driver was standing beside it, grinning broadly and taking in every word they exchanged.

Ben stared helplessly toward the driver, who merely shrugged. "I'm on her clock now," he told Ben. "She wants these back here, I'll put 'em back in the studio."

"Go ahead," Ben said, defeated.

Struggling to figure out what the devil had gone so wildly wrong, Ben turned back to Kathleen. "I thought you wanted to do a showing. Isn't that what the last past few months have been about?"

She hauled off and slugged him. "You are such an idiot," she said, then stomped past him and went inside to watch as the driver unloaded the last of the paintings.

Ben followed, rubbing his stinging jaw. As soon as they were alone, he asked, "Did I get it wrong? You don't want to do a show?"

"Of course I do, but not like this. Not if it's some sort of weird trade-off for sex," she said furiously. "Or, just as bad, a way to buy yourself a little peace of mind and get me out of your life, now that you've satisfied that itch I stirred in you."

To his shame, he could see exactly how she could leap to such a tawdry conclusion. He'd never told her how he felt, never admitted that he'd come to trust her...that he loved her. How could he, when he was terrified by the admission?

He could see from the flash of fury in her eyes that if he didn't find the words, he was going to lose her. Besides, what difference did the words make, really? The feeling was there, in his heart, every time he looked at her. It was too late to stop that. There was no way to take it back, to protect himself. He'd only deluded himself into thinking that sending those paintings would put an end to things.

He remembered the very recent conversation with his brothers and forced himself to keep his eye on the only goal that really mattered. Then he drew in a deep breath and looked into her eyes.

"What if they were a wedding gift, from me to you?" he asked, watching closely for her reaction.

She blinked rapidly. "What?"

He grinned at her confusion, at the hint of hope that burned in her eyes. "I'm trying to propose here and making a mess of it. I should have asked Destiny to write a proper speech for me."

"I think Destiny's been involved a little too much in this already," she responded. She stepped close, rested a gentle hand against his still-burning cheek. Her eyes were soft and misty. "You're doing fine on your own. A few little words, Ben. That's all I need to hear."

"The pictures are yours?"

She frowned at his teasing. "Not even close."

"I trust you with my art, with my life."

She nodded. "Better."

He took a deep breath. "I love you, Kathleen. I want to marry you, raise a family with you, wake up with you every morning till we're both old and gray."

"Bingo." She stood on tiptoe and kissed him. "Was that so hard?"

"Yes," he told her honestly. "It scares the hell out of me."

"It'll get easier," she promised. "You're going to have a lifetime to practice."

A lifetime. The word echoed in his head and he

waited for the panic to follow. Instead he was filled with incomparable joy. He'd finally gotten it right. About damn time. He wouldn't mind staying right here and sealing this deal with something far more intimate than a kiss, but there was someplace the two of them needed to be.

"Much as I'd like to hang around here and keep on practicing, there's a little matter of a baby who's about to arrive," he told her. "If this baby is anything like its daddy, it's bound to be impatient, now that it's decided the time is right."

She stared at him in shock. "Melanie and Richard's baby?"

He nodded.

"*That's* why he and Mack went tearing out of here just as I arrived! I thought they just didn't want to stick around for the inevitable fireworks," she said, then scowled at him. "Why didn't you say something sooner? You need to be at the hospital."

"I've barely gotten a word in edgewise since you got here," he reminded her. "Well, except for the proposal. I did fit that in. Anyway, we need to be there. You're going to be part of this family now."

A slow smile spread across her face. "How soon?"

He chuckled. "Are you in a hurry for some reason?"

"I want to be your wife when I open this show in my gallery." At his shocked look, she added, "You don't get to take them back now, buster. You gave them to me as a wedding present, and I don't want any other woman thinking she can poach on the sexiest artist in the United States."

"And you want to do this show when?" he asked, amused by her eagerness.

"January," she said at once. "February at the latest."

He laughed at that. "Destiny's counting on a June wedding."

"Well, she's just going to have to be disappointed," Kathleen said adamantly. "She's gotten her way with everything else. We're picking the wedding date."

"Seems fair enough to me. You can talk about it at the hospital."

"Let's go," she said eagerly, heading for her car.

"Kathleen!"

She turned back. "What?"

He gestured toward her car. "Not a chance in hell. We'll take mine."

She laughed. "Mine's closer."

"Then I'll drive."

"What's wrong with my driving?" she asked, even as she docilely went around to the passenger side of the car.

"Too fast and too dangerous," he said succinctly. He decided it was time to lay his greatest fear on the table, the one he couldn't shake because he was reminded of it every single time he saw her behind the wheel. "It reminds me of the way Graciela drove."

Her mouth dropped open and tears immediately filled her eyes. "Oh, Ben, why didn't you say something? I thought you were just being a macho jerk."

He shrugged. "Maybe a little of that, too," he admitted. "Think you can slow down, just enough so I don't go crazy worrying every time you're on the road?"

She reached for his hand. "I'll never go above the speed limit again," she promised.

"That's something, I suppose."

"You wouldn't want me to poke along, would you?"

"It would make my day, actually."

"Then I'll drive like some little old lady heading for church on Sunday," she promised. "You're not going to lose me in an accident, Ben. Not if I can help it."

"I wish it were possible to be sure of that," he told her. "But I know it's not. I just know I don't want to lose you by pretending that I don't love you."

She touched his cheek. "Then isn't it a good thing you've admitted it at last? We've got that all cleared up."

"Yes," he said quietly. "It's a very good thing."

The best, in fact.

At the hospital they found Destiny, Mack and Beth gathered in the waiting room. There was no sign of Richard.

"Did he faint?" Ben asked.

"No, he's in the delivery room," Mack said. "Pity the poor doctor with Richard looking over his shoulder. I'm sure he had a plan for just how this delivery is supposed to go, too."

Kathleen and Beth exchanged a look and chuckled.

"Fortunately, Dr. Kelly has dealt with a great many expectant fathers before," Beth said confidently. "I think he can keep Richard in line."

"Ha!" Mack said. "Richard is used to running a multinational corporation. Organizing a delivery room to suit him will be a piece of cake."

"Not after the first time Melanie screams her head off," Beth predicted.

Mack paled at that. "There's going to be screaming?"

"Plenty, I imagine," Beth confirmed.

He scowled at her. "We are adopting all of our kids."

Beth gave him a long, lingering look, then said quietly, "Too late for that."

Mack simply stared at her. "A baby," he said eventually. "We're going to have a baby?"

"In about eight months," Beth said, grinning.

Mack sank onto a chair as Kathleen and Destiny rushed over to hug Beth. Ben went to sit beside his obviously shaken brother.

"You okay?" Ben asked.

Mack nodded slowly. "I didn't know about the screaming."

"Can't be much worse than some football player who's just gotten his collar bone dislocated." He gave Mack a pointed look. "Or his knee shattered."

"I didn't scream," Mack said defensively. "Either time."

"Tell that to someone who couldn't hear you from twenty rows up on the fifty-yard line," Ben said. "Women have been doing this since time began. They're tough. Tougher than we are, in fact."

Mack glanced over in the direction of his wife and smiled slowly. "Yeah, they are, aren't they?" He turned back to Ben. "So what about you and Kathleen? Did you work things out?"

"We're getting married," Ben admitted.

"Well, hallelujah!"

His exuberant shout brought the three women across the room.

"More good news?" Beth asked, her gaze on Ben.

He glanced at Kathleen. "Looks like we're all going to steal the new baby's thunder."

"I seriously doubt Richard or Melanie will even notice," Beth told him. "Come on, spill it."

"I asked Kathleen to marry me," he said, reaching for her hand. "And she's said yes."

Destiny began to cry. "Now that is worth celebrating. Oh, darling, I am so happy for you. For both of you." She sighed. "A June wedding will be perfect."

"Not June," Kathleen told her without apology. "January."

Destiny's mouth gaped. "This January? As in next month?"

"That's what she said," Ben confirmed. "Before my show opens at her gallery."

Destiny sank onto the chair next to Mack and reached for his hand. "Well, this really is moving along quickly."

Ben caught an odd note in her voice. "Too quickly?" he asked worriedly.

"Oh no, darling. Getting you happily settled could never come too quickly."

"Then why did you say that?" he asked.

"Never mind," she said briskly and turned her attention to Kathleen. "We have a lot to do. I think we should get your mother down here right away, don't you?"

Kathleen paled. "Oh, my God. I forgot all about going to Providence." She glanced at her watch. "They're going to be expecting me any minute now."

"Call them," Destiny advised. "Tell them about the baby and the engagement and invite them all to come here tomorrow. I can't imagine a better way to celebrate Christmas. We have so much happy news."

"You know, you could be right," Kathleen said. "Maybe this will be enough to get them all to finally come down here. I'll go outside and call right now on my cell phone."

Ben followed her. "You sure you want to drop this bombshell on them like this?" he asked. "We could go up there tomorrow. Maybe they should at least meet me before we spring the rest of the family on them."

"No," she said decisively. "I like the idea of all of us being together here on Christmas. Maybe they'll see what a real family holiday can be like."

"Whatever you want," he said. "Want me to wait for you inside?"

She reached for his hand. "No, stay with me," she pleaded as the call went through. "Hello, Mother."

Ben couldn't hear exactly what her mother said, but it was communicated in an aggrieved tone he couldn't mistake. He watched Kathleen intently, but her expression never wavered.

"Mother, if you'll just listen for a minute, I can explain. I got engaged tonight, to Ben Carlton, the artist I told you about, the man in my painting."

Her expression softened at whatever her mother said then. "Yes, it is wonderful news. And there's more. His brother's wife is in the hospital right now having a baby, and we want to stay for that, but Destiny's invited all of you for Christmas dinner tomorrow. Will you come? Please."

Relief spread over her face. "I'll call grandfather with the directions, then. Thank you, Mother. I love you and Merry Christmas."

She turned off the cell phone and stood staring at it, tears shimmering in her eyes.

"I gather she said yes," Ben said.

Kathleen nodded. "She says she can't wait to meet all of you." She grinned. "She also said she knew it was inevitable from the minute she saw the portrait of you.''

''Really? Wonder what she'll say when she sees the one I've painted of you,'' he said, glad that he'd hidden it away before sending the shipment to her gallery.

Kathleen's mouth gaped. ''You painted a portrait of me?''

''In the moonlight,'' he confirmed.

''Oh, sweet heaven,'' she murmured, her cheeks turning pink. ''Do I have any clothes on?''

''Enough,'' he told her, laughing. ''Too many to suit me, though, but I wanted our kids to be able to look at this and see you the way I see you.''

''I want to see it,'' she said at once.

''You will,'' he promised. ''But right now we'd better get back inside and see what kind of progress that baby is making.''

It was one minute after midnight when Amelia Destiny Carlton arrived, the Christmas baby that Beth had predicted. Destiny's eyes shone with tears when she heard the baby's name.

''You didn't have to do that,'' she whispered, clutching Richard's hand.

''We wanted to,'' Melanie said. ''If it weren't for you, none of this would ever have happened.''

''Amen to that,'' Mack agreed, his gaze on Beth.

She smiled and tucked her hand into his. ''I predict a lot of little Destinys in this family before too long.''

''I am not naming any boy of mine Destiny,'' Mack grumbled.

''And if it's another girl?'' Ben asked him.

''That's different,'' Mack said, giving their aunt a hug.

Ben gazed at the tiny, perfect little girl in Richard's

arms. He glanced back at Kathleen. "I wonder if I can get that portrait finished in time for the show?"

They all stared at him.

"You're painting portraits now?" Melanie asked.

"And showing your work?" Richard echoed.

Ben laughed at their shocked expressions. "Oh, yeah, that's right, you were out of the room when I mentioned that I'm also getting married."

"Oh, sweetie, that's wonderful," Melanie said and began to cry. She swiped at her eyes. "Don't mind me. Hormones."

"Hormones nothing," Richard scoffed. "You're just sentimental."

"I notice you've got tears in your eyes, too, bro," Mack commented.

Richard shrugged. "What the hell! I'd say the Carlton men have come a long way, wouldn't you?"

"A very long way," Melanie and Beth agreed.

Destiny gazed at each of them in turn, then clucked her tongue. "Don't encourage them too much, ladies. There's always room for a little improvement."

Ben picked his aunt up and twirled her around until she told him he was making her dizzy.

"Not until you promise to stop meddling," he said. "Your work here is done, Destiny."

She gave him a long look that was tinged with just a hint of sorrow. "Yes, it is, isn't it?"

"Oh, no, it's not," Melanie piped up.

"Absolutely not," Kathleen and Beth agreed. "There's a whole new generation to worry about now."

To Ben's relief, Destiny's expression brightened. "My goodness, I can't leave this precious baby and all the ones to come to the likes of you, can I?"

"Hey!" Richard protested. "I don't think we turned out too badly."

"Neither do I," Mack said.

Ben looked at his brothers and the women in their lives, then turned to Kathleen. "What about you? Do you think I've turned out all right?"

She moved into his arms and pressed a kiss to his cheek, then whispered in his ear, "I wouldn't want the others to hear this, but I think you turned out best of all."

"You're biased."

She laughed. "Hey, I'm only following Destiny's lead. Everybody knows you're her favorite."

"I heard that," Richard grumbled.

"Me, too," Mack protested.

"Oh, stop squabbling," Destiny said. "I don't have favorites."

"Of course not," Ben agreed at once, then leaned down. "But if you did, I'd be the one, right?"

"Isn't knowing that you're Kathleen's favorite enough?" Destiny scolded.

Ben met Kathleen's gaze over Destiny's head. "More than enough," he agreed at once. It was something he would never allow himself to forget.

Epilogue

For a wedding that had been pulled together in less than a month, Kathleen thought it was pretty spectacular. Her mother and Destiny had used every contact, called in every favor and invited a cast of hundreds to witness the occasion. She didn't think it could have come together any more beautifully if they'd had an entire year to plan it.

Kathleen stood at the back of the church in a sleek, strapless satin gown from a well-known designer whom Destiny knew personally. She was holding a simple bouquet of lily of the valley and white velvet ribbons that her mother had created. Her grandfather, looking incredibly distinguished in his tuxedo, stood at her side.

"Are you happy, angel? Truly happy?" he asked.

"You can't begin to imagine how happy," she assured him. "I've gotten it exactly right this time."

"I hope so. Ben seems like a fine young man and

it's plain that he adores you. I don't suppose you'd reconsider and settle in Providence?"

She squeezed his hand. "No, but it means the world to me that you'd want us to."

He nodded, his expression sad. "I wish I'd done better by you and your mother."

"That's in the past, Grandfather, and it has nothing to do with me wanting to stay here. My life is here now."

He patted her hand. "No need to explain. Now it seems to me that I hear music. Are you ready?"

"I've been waiting my whole life for this," she said as they took their places at the back of the church and waited for Melanie and Beth to reach the front.

"Let's do it," she said eagerly as the organ music swelled.

Then she had eyes only for Ben, who was standing in front of the altar, Mack and Richard beside him. Destiny was in the front pew, tears streaming down her face as she watched Kathleen come down the aisle.

When Kathleen reached Ben's aunt, she impulsively leaned down and kissed her cheek, then crossed the aisle and kissed her mother. "Thank you both," she murmured before stepping into place beside Ben.

Ben solemnly shook her grandfather's hand, then reached over to clasp hers. His grip was solid and comforting, the grip of a man who finally knew his heart and was ready to reach out to grab the future.

"I love you," he mouthed silently as the minister began the ceremony.

Kathleen beamed at him. Once he'd started saying the words, it seemed he hadn't been able to say them often enough, which suited her just fine. If they lived to be a hundred, she would never tire of hearing them.

* * *

"Okay, Destiny, the wedding's over," Richard said not five minutes after the ceremony, even though the photographer was impatiently waiting for them to gather for pictures. "You said you'd tell me your idea about dealing with William Harcourt once Ben and Kathleen were married."

Destiny gave him a look that would have daunted most men, but Richard was a Carlton. He simply stared right back at her and waited.

"Oh, for goodness' sakes," she snapped finally. "You're not going to let this alone, so I might as well tell you." She turned to Ben and Kathleen. "Sorry, dears, but if I don't get this over with, he'll spoil your reception by dogging my every footstep."

"Please, Destiny, go ahead," Kathleen told her. She was actually anxious to hear this scheme herself. It was bound to be a doozy.

Destiny looked each of her nephews in the eye, then said with quiet determination. "I intend to take over the European division of Carlton Industries," she said. "I will deal with William. In fact, I predict it will be some time before he knows what's hit him."

With that, she turned and walked away, back straight, shoulders squared, looking for all the world as if she were heading into battle.

Kathleen was the first to break the silence. She began to chuckle.

"What's so blasted funny?" Ben demanded.

"I agree," Richard said, his expression grim. "I don't find this the least bit amusing."

"Oh, chill, big brother," Mack said. "I think Kathleen's right. This is perfect retribution."

"On who? Us?" Ben asked irritably.

"No. On William. If you think it was fun watching the three of you squirm while she was matchmaking," Kathleen responded, "something tells me this is going to be a whole lot more entertaining."

"Absolutely," Beth agreed.

"Oh, yes," Melanie added happily.

Ben turned a sour look on all the women. "Good God, they're all ganging up on us now. I knew there was a downside to adding all these women to the family. We're outnumbered now."

Kathleen laughed at his dismay. "And don't you forget it," she said cheerfully. "But we do love you."

"Most of the time," Melanie added.

Beth gazed pointedly at Mack. "When you're not trying to control things."

He held up his hand. "Hey, have this baby on your own. I won't hover."

"That'll be the day," Beth said. "Now come on. We have pictures to be taken and a reception to get to before the guests eat all the food."

Melanie grinned at her. "Appetite growing, Beth?"

"By leaps and bounds. If this keeps up, I'll be waddling around the hospital by my fifth month."

"I told you I could give you an exercise regimen," Mack said.

Ben and Richard immediately hooted. "Oh, brother, please tell me you didn't say that," Richard said.

"What's wrong?" Mack asked. "I'm trying to be helpful."

"Keep it up and you'll be a dead man," Beth warned.

Kathleen turned to Ben. "I hope you're taking all this in," she told him. "That way when I'm pregnant, you'll have all the dos and don'ts down pat."

"I already have a plan," he assured her. "I'm moving out of the country."

She pulled his face down and kissed him hard. "Not a chance. You're never leaving my side, so get that idea right out of your head."

"Like I said, I'll stay and keep my mouth shut."

"There you go," she said happily.

If he'd learned that lesson already, they were destined for a very joyous marriage.

* * * * *

*Watch for a brand-new
miniseries by Sherryl Woods,*
ROSE COTTAGE,
*on sale in February 2005,
from Silhouette Special Edition.
And now turn the page
for a sneak preview of Sherryl Woods's
exciting new novel,*
DESTINY UNLEASHED,
*in which the matchmaking Aunt Destiny
finds* her *match.
On sale in June 2004
from MIRA Books*

"**Y**ou want to do what?" Richard's head snapped up from the stack of papers on his desk. He studied his aunt as if she'd announced an intention to take up sky-diving, though come to think of it that was something Destiny was entirely likely to do if boredom set in. This announcement was far more unexpected.

"Don't glower at me like that," she scolded. "I told you weeks ago I planned this. It's not as if I haven't grown up around this company. I know its inner workings almost as well as you do. It was my grandfather who started it, after all, and my father who turned it into a world-wide conglomerate. I've held a seat on the board for years now and, believe me, I do not let the reports sit on my desk gathering dust. I may be the only person on the board besides you who actually reads them."

"But you've never shown the slightest interest in working for Carlton Industries," Richard said, totally perplexed. "When your father tried to groom you for a position here, you ran away to France. When you came back after my father died, you left it to his executive vice president to run things until I was old enough to take over."

"Because, just like you, your father lived and breathed this company. I simply let him have it because it was the sensible, fair thing to do. I had more interesting things to pursue. And when I came back, I had far more important responsibilities—you and your brothers. The company was running smoothly and you were already being groomed to take over. There was no need for my interference or involvement.''

''Okay, I can accept all that,'' he said, still perplexed. ''What's changed?''

''I've changed,'' she said simply. ''Now I want to run the European division. If you agree to this, Richard, I can promise you won't regret it.''

''But why?'' Richard persisted.

''Because it's there,'' she snapped impatiently. ''Don't be dense, Richard. I want to do it because now that you and your brothers are married, I need something to do. I want to find out what I'm really made of.''

He was still bewildered. His aunt's days were jampacked with things to do. ''When was the last time your calendar wasn't crammed with foundation meetings, fund-raisers, luncheons and social engagements?''

Destiny waved them off as if they were of no consequence. ''There was a time when that life-style suited me. Now it doesn't. I need a real purpose. I want to make a contribution to this family. I think I have something unique to offer Carlton Industries. All those years coaxing dollars out of tightwads for various charities ought to be good for something.''

''Hold it right there,'' Richard said, regarding her with exasperation. ''Don't you think you made an incredible contribution by coming back here to take over when Mom and Dad died? You gave the three of us a home and stability. You brought fun and adventure into our lives. Rosalind Russell in that old *Auntie Mame* movie you showed us had nothing on you. You saw that we became decent, well-educated men. Hell, you even meddled until we were married to women you approved of. There's a whole new generation of Carltons coming along, thanks to you.''

''Exactly my point,'' Destiny responded. ''You're all settled. You have your own families. You don't need me anymore.''

''We'll always need you,'' Richard protested, indignant that she could think otherwise. ''Have we not shown you that?''

''You need me as the doting great-aunt who spoils your children rotten, nothing more. I can't be content with that. I want more.''

He decided to try another tack to dissuade her from this insane idea. ''What about your house in France? I always thought you'd want to go back there someday to live, get back to your painting and your gardens. You always talk about that time in your life as if it were magical. Now's your chance. Go for a few months. Open your studio and paint again.''

''All that's in the past,'' she said blithely, as if she hadn't talked incessantly about doing that very thing at some distant point in the future. ''You can't recapture something that was lost. In fact, I'm thinking of selling the house.''

Shocked by the blasé announcement, he stared at her. ''Now I know there's something wrong. What aren't you telling me? You always swore you would never sell that house, that you wanted to know it was there for your old age.''

She shrugged. ''Times change. I was young and impetuous back then. While you boys were growing up, so was I. I have new dreams now.''

Richard regarded her skeptically. "And one of those dreams is to run our European division?"

"Yes," she declared flatly.

Truthfully, he didn't doubt for a second that she could do it. Destiny was an amazing woman. She had a huge and generous heart, an astounding zest for life, and a mind that could grasp the details of a business merger even more quickly than his.

In her fifties, she was still a beautiful woman, trim and lithe with a cloud of soft brown hair framing a face that time had treated kindly. Her generous mouth was usually curved in a brilliant smile and laugh lines fanned out from eyes that sparkled.

There was no shortage of available men to fill her evenings, and yet she kept most of them at arm's length. His wife said it was because Destiny still longed for the love of her life, the man she'd left behind when she'd come home to take charge of her nephews. Maybe that was true, though Richard didn't like thinking that she'd sacrificed someone so irreplaceable that she'd spent the past twenty years yearning for him. It would be even worse if that man turned out to be William Harcourt, the very man who'd become the bane of Richard's existence by mucking about in every deal Carlton Industries tried to make in Europe.

He pushed all of that from his mind and tried to view this request from Destiny's perspective. In all these years she had never asked for anything for herself. She'd thrown herself into sudden and unexpected motherhood with complete abandon, mastering it with her own unorthodox style. If she wanted this one thing from him now, how could he deny her?

Still, the decision seemed so impulsive, so out of character, he had to be sure it wasn't a whim. Carlton

Industries wasn't some playground for a woman who was simply bored with her life.

"Destiny, have you really thought this through?" he asked. "There are downsides. Tackling such a huge job will mean long days. There will be a lot of stress involved."

Her gaze narrowed. "Are you suggesting I'm not physically or mentally up to it?" she asked, her tone suddenly icy.

Richard knew better than to say any such thing. "Of course not."

"Well then, why are you hesitating?"

"Because this is so unlike you. In fact, every time I've brought up the European division and the problems it was having, you've told me to deal with it myself."

She regarded him blandly. "But you haven't, have you?"

Richard sighed. She had him there. William Harcourt was still injecting himself into every single negotiation Carlton Industries was involved in. Richard had managed to thwart most of Harcourt's attempts to steal business, but he hadn't really dealt the man a final, knockout blow that would end the nonsense.

He couldn't help wondering yet again if there was a link between Harcourt and Destiny he didn't know about. He'd asked Destiny before if she had known the man years ago, but she'd avoided giving him a direct answer. Ben had managed to finagle an admission that she'd known Harcourt, but had gotten nothing more. That rather incomplete acknowledgment had raised Richard's suspicions that there was more going on with Harcourt than business, but without proof he hadn't been able to call her on it. He needed to try again.

"Does this have something to do with Harcourt?" he asked her.

"No, it has to do with me," she insisted, regarding him with an unblinking gaze that gave away nothing. "It's time to find out what I'm made of."

"You're an incredible woman!" Richard said impatiently. "Why are you questioning that now? Don't start spouting some nonsense about low self-esteem to me. I'll laugh you right out of here."

"Darling, it's not that I don't think I did a good job raising you and your brothers or that I haven't made a contribution to the community, but I don't know who I am, not really. Somewhere along the way I've lost myself."

Richard was completely bewildered by her claim. "That's crazy."

"Is it? I was very young when I first went to Europe. I had plenty of money and virtually no responsibilities. I painted because I enjoyed it, not because I was passionate about it. I was surrounded by people who were as irresponsible as I was."

"Including William Harcourt?" he asked again, wondering if she would finally give him an honest answer.

She gave him a sour look. "Yes, if you must know, including William."

When Richard would have pressed her on that, she held up her hand. "The point I'm trying to make is that when your parents died, I came back here and had the responsibility of a family thrust on me. I think I lived up to that responsibility reasonably well—"

"Of course you did."

"But," she added with a trace of impatience, "those years were a gift, something unexpected, that shaped

my life for a time, but now I'm ready to move on. I
need to find out who Destiny Carlton really is.''

"And you think you could be a successful businesswoman?''

"Why not?'' she asked. "It is in my genes, after
all.'' She gave him a hard look. "I honestly don't know
why you're making such a fuss or why you're so surprised by this. I've been talking about it for months
now, ever since Ben's wedding.''

"I honestly didn't think you were serious.''

"In other words, you were certain it was just another
one of Destiny's flighty whims,'' she scoffed. "And
that says it all, doesn't it? Is it any wonder I want my
family, of all people, to start to take me seriously?''

He could see that he'd hurt her, but he didn't know
how else he could have reacted to this crazy idea. He
couldn't just turn over an entire division to her because
it was what she wanted. He had as much responsibility
to the company as he did to her.

"Destiny, why don't you think it over for another
day or two? Or take a vacation, go to France again and
see if that fits you the way it once did,'' he suggested
finally, hoping to buy himself enough time to formulate
a plan to steer all this energy in some other direction.
Surely there was some other satisfying pursuit she
could take up that would keep her right here at home.
Maybe they could encourage her to accept one of the
marriage proposals constantly being tossed her way by
high-profile men in the region. The prospect of a little
turnabout meddling struck him as a fine idea.

Meantime, though, he gave her a placating smile.
"Think about it for a few days or even a few weeks
and we'll talk again.''

"Meaning you want to check with your brothers to

make sure I haven't gone round the bend,'' she said dryly. "Okay, fine. I'll compromise. I won't put this off for weeks, but I can wait twenty-four hours while you hold a family powwow, as long as it gets me what I want. Trust me, Richard, I won't change my mind.''

It wasn't the delay he'd hoped for, but he could see she wasn't prepared to bend any further. "Fine. We'll get together at the end of the day tomorrow.''

She gave him an innocent look. "I really hope you'll see this my way,'' she said cheerfully. "I'd hate to have to waste my time pulling rank on you and going straight to the board to explain that the European operation has been in a shambles for some time and that you haven't taken any definitive action to shore it up and turn it into the gold mine it could be.''

As her words sank in, Richard stared at her. If he had ever doubted her business acumen or her ability to be a tough negotiator, he didn't any longer. She'd obviously done her homework before coming to him. And she'd delivered that threat without so much as a blink of her steady gaze.

"You would do that?'' he asked, stunned by her audacity.

She beamed at him. "I don't think it will be necessary, do you?''

With that Destiny swept out of his office looking as regal and smug as a queen.

Richard watched her exit and sighed. Heaven help the European division! There was little doubt that Destiny was taking over. He considered himself to be a tough-minded businessman and a seasoned negotiator, but she'd put him in his place in no time flat. He'd just have to find some way to keep her on a tight rein.

But even as he reached that conclusion, Richard had to laugh. Keeping his aunt under control was going to be a little like trying to contain a hurricane. It simply couldn't be done.

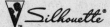

SPECIAL EDITION™

MILLION DOLLAR DESTINIES

Three brothers discover
all the riches money can't buy.

**A delightful new series
from *USA TODAY* bestselling author**

SHERRYL WOODS

ISN'T IT RICH?
(Silhouette Special Edition #1597, on sale March 2004)

PRICELESS
(Silhouette Special Edition #1603, on sale April 2004)

TREASURED
(Silhouette Special Edition #1609, on sale May 2004)

And don't miss...

DESTINY UNLEASHED
a *Million Dollar Destinies* story
on sale June 2004 from MIRA Books.

Available at your favorite retail outlet.

Visit Silhouette at www.eHarlequin.com   SSEMDDMINI

eHARLEQUIN.com

For **FREE online reading,** visit
www.eHarlequin.com now and enjoy:

<u>Online Reads</u>
Read **Daily** and **Weekly** chapters from
our Internet-exclusive stories by your
favorite authors.

<u>Red-Hot Reads</u>
Turn up the heat with one of our more
sensual online stories!

<u>Interactive Novels</u>
Cast your vote to help decide how these
stories unfold...then stay tuned!

<u>Quick Reads</u>
For shorter romantic reads, try our
collection of Poems, Toasts, & More!

<u>Online Read Library</u>
Miss one of our online reads?
Come here to catch up!

<u>Reading Groups</u>
Discuss, share and rave with other
community members!

For great reading online,
visit www.eHarlequin.com today!

INTONL

A peaceful Southern town.
A terrible evil.
The power of silence.

**From *USA TODAY*
bestselling author**

ERICA SPINDLER

Journalist Avery Chauvin is devastated
to hear that her father has taken his
own life. Disbelieving and desperate
to find answers, Avery returns to
Cypress Springs, Louisiana, where she
hears rumors of strange happenings.
And in her father's house she finds a
box of fifteen-year-old newspaper
articles, each covering the brutal
murder of a local woman.

Then the past and present collide. A
woman is found savagely murdered.
An outsider passing through town
vanishes. And Avery begins to wonder,
could her father have been murdered?

IN SILENCE

"Readers will be pulled
inexorably onward by the
question of whodunit."
—*Publishers Weekly*

*Available May 2004
wherever paperbacks are sold.*

Visit us at www.mirabooks.com

MES2037

Silhouette®

SPECIAL EDITION™

After *The Sons of Caitlin Bravo* comes...

BRAVO FAMILY TIES

Stronger Than Ever

From award-winning author

Christine Rimmer

FIFTY WAYS TO SAY... I'M PREGNANT

(Silhouette Special Edition #1615)

Starr Bravo had been in love with rancher Beau Tisdale since she was sixteen, yet they'd agreed that this "summer of love" was just that. When September rolled around, they'd go their separate ways—she to her glamorous job in New York City, he back to the ranch.

But now she needed to get the words out— Beau, I'm pregnant—before their baby did it for her!

Available June 2004
at your favorite retail outlet.

Visit Silhouette Books at www.eHarlequin.com

SSEFWTSIP

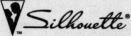

COMING NEXT MONTH

SPECIAL EDITION

#1615 FIFTY WAYS TO SAY I'M PREGNANT—Christine Rimmer
Bravo Family Ties
Reunited after six long years, Starr Bravo and Beau Tisdale couldn't
deny the attraction that had always sizzled between
them. But when Starr discovered she was carrying Beau's baby,
she panicked and fled the scene. Could Beau find—and forgive—
his one true love so they could be a family at last?

#1616 ACCIDENTAL FAMILY—Joan Elliott Pickart
The Baby Bet: MacAllister's Gifts
When Patty Sharpe Clark set out to track down a child's missing
father, David Montgomery, she was shocked to learn he'd been
in an accident and had amnesia! She vowed to care for Sarah Ann
until the girl's father recovered, but would Patty find love where she
least expected?

#1617 CAVANAUGH'S WOMAN—Marie Ferrarella
Cavanaugh Justice
Deeply dedicated to his family and work, Shaw Cavanaugh didn't
have time for the frivolity of life…until he met Moira McCormick.
The charming actress came from a troubled past and longed to be
part of a family, but would Shaw accept her into his life…forever?

#1618 HOT AUGUST NIGHTS—Christine Flynn
The Kendricks of Camelot
After CEO Matt Callaway and Ashley Kendrick shared a steamy
one-night stand, the fear of scandal had separated them. Ashley had
never forgotten the way Matt made her feel, but would he be able to
forgive her for keeping their unborn child a secret…?

#1619 THE DADDY SURVEY—Janis Reams Hudson
Men of Cherokee Rose
Rancher Sloan Chisolm had never turned his back on a woman in
trouble. So when beautiful Emily Nelson lost her job as a waitress,
he was determined that she come work for him at the Cherokee
Rose Ranch. He knew she considered being his housekeeper
temporary, but their kisses made him hope that this might be a
partnership…for life.

#1620 ONE PERFECT MAN—Lynda Sandoval
Years ago Tomas Garza's dreams of a family had fallen apart after
his wife abandoned him and their daughter. He'd desperately tried
to fill the void in his daughter's life, but the time had come when
she needed a woman—someone like the beautiful event planner
Erica Goncalves. She'd agreed to help him plan a party for his
daughter, but would she be open to something more permanent?